Nightshift

by

Dave Leigh.

Introduction.

I don't know about you but whenever I read a book, it's almost as though I'm watching it as a film in my head. I think that is the way that this book must be read.

Follow the adventures and misadventures of a group of cops in England as they work through various shifts in the early 2000's.

And, yes, there's a little bit of social commentary about Policing and Society thrown in as well that still stands today.

I cannot confirm or deny if any of the events in this book actually happened, I'll let you make your own minds up. It is totally accidental (honest) if any of the characters resemble anyone serving or retired.

If my comments offend a particular group or department please remember one word - Banter.

Apologies to the people of St Helens as I've made up street names where there is an actual address in the story and sometimes I've grossly over exaggerated how an area is simply to set the scene.

The attitudes and behaviours displayed in this book are those that were around at that time and not a reflection of those in Policing today.

I almost called this book TJF (The Job's Fucked) a reference only those in the job would understand, but it is explained in the content of the book.

I'm not a professional author so I've written this in a style that I find easy to read and I hope it works for you too. I'd describe it as a quasi-documentary style (is that even a thing or have I just made that up?) I don't do 2 page descriptions of a vase on a mantelpiece to take up space. The stories are direct and to the point. Part of it was originally written as a script for a TV show idea and, to me, it still reads a little that way.

WARNING. Some of the events in this book may act as 'triggers' for some people. If that does happen please, please, please talk about it and seek help.

And a little quote that, to me, sums up Policing on the front line: "We trained hard, but it seemed that every time we were beginning to form up into teams we would be reorganised. I was to learn later in life that we tend to meet any new situation by reorganising: And a wonderful method it can be for creating the illusion of progress, while producing confusion, inefficiency and demoralisation."

Caius Petronius, Roman Consul 66A.D.

"No fucking change there then."

Anonymous St Helens Constable 2008.

This book is dedicated to my wife and son *and* the brave men and women in blue who run towards danger when others run away.

First Nightshift.

Thursday

2200hrs.

In the station.

Dan and Ken are going to play a trick on Chris, one of the probationers on the block

Dan is an overweight white male in his mid-twenties about 6ft tall, short ginger hair. He has been in the Police for about 5 years and is still learning his trade.

Ken is a white male in his early forties of average build and about 5ft 10 in tall, short dark hair that is greying at the sides. He's been in the Police for 15years and can be quite jaded in his attitude at times and have strong opinions.

Chris is a white male of athletic build in his early twenties, about 6ft tall, blonde hair that is shaved close to his skull. He is still within his probationary period of the initial 2 years in the Police.

Chris has been given the job of Station Keeper working the front desk for the night.

As is the tradition they have brought a brew down for the Station Keeper who cannot leave the front desk.

1

Ken is keeping Chris talking whilst Dan sets up the prank.

In the corridor outside the front office, Ken sounding interested: "So how are things going, Chris, keeping up with the paperwork?"

Chris, thinking that Ken is genuinely interested: "Yeah not too bad, if it isn't too busy I've got the chance to catch up on a few traffic accident files I need to write off."

Ken, with a bit of fake sympathy: "Bloody hate dealing with accident files, it's always a godsend to old sweats like me when we've got a probie on the Block cos you lot get the majority of them."

Chris: "Yeah, it's not fair really."

Ken: "Got to put up with stuff like that until you've got your 2 years in mate. Equips you for when you are on your own."

In the front office Dan is working away on his hands and knees doing something under the swivel/adjustable chair by the computer terminal.

He's taping an air horn underneath the chair.

Dan comes out of the office.

Dan: "Alright, Chris, cocker, I've left your brew on the desk. 2 sugars innit?"

Chris: "Yeah, nice one mate."

Dan and Ken head off down the corridor.

Chris enters the front office, picks up his brew and takes a big slurp then, cup still in hand, plonks himself down in the chair whereupon there is an almighty blast of the air horn.

Chris jumps out of his skin, flying back to his feet, spilling his brew all over himself.

Dan and Ken are at the end of the corridor almost wetting themselves with laughter.

From inside the front office.

Chris: "You pair of bastards!"

Ken and Dan scarper off down the corridor, laughing.

2230hrs.

Ken and Dan are on patrol.

Dan: "What do you think of the new Boss then?"

Ken: "Remains to be seen mate. After 15 years, I've only had a handful of good bosses."

Dan: "Really mate? A few who joined with me are starting to go up the promotion ladder, decent types."

Ken: "Wait and see, it changes them when they start chasing promotion. Some of them will do anything to get that next rank up. They'll step on anyone who gets in their way, and happily steal ideas

3

to rebrand them as their own, just to look good to those higher up or to use as evidence to say how good they are."

Dan: "What about this new fella then?"

Ken: "Stayed in his office all last shift didn't he? Doesn't bode well."

Dan: "I see what you mean."

Ken: "I'll tell you what though, he's a big fella, give you a run for your money at the table."

Dan is outraged. "Bollocks, no one can shovel it down like me!"

Ken: "I heard on the grapevine that he's a bit of a Walter Mitty character as well."

Dan's puzzled: "What's one of them?"

Ken: "You know the type? If you came in and said you'd climbed Everest, he'd say he'd done that years ago ...twice"

Dan, nodding sagely: "Ah, bit of a Billy Bullshitter then."

Ken: "Apparently so, and I've heard he'll stitch you up at the drop of a hat to make himself look good. Bit of a brown noser to those higher up."

0030hrs.

Dan and Ken are on patrol.

Radio: "Delta Mike 1 1 can you make to a report of a Sudden Death, please? 25 West End Street, relatives have entered property and found their mother passed away."

Ken: "Yeah, roger will do."

Dan, vehemently: "Fuckin hell mate, I hate dealing with dead bodies, freaks me out. Do you mind taking the lead on this one?"

Ken, "No probs, mate."

0040hrs.

Dan and Ken arrive at scene, a long row of terraced houses, the kind of 2 up 2 down houses that you see all over the country.

They get out of the Police car and approach the front door which is open slightly.

Ken knocks and they enter the house where a male and female in their 20's are in the living room.

The décor is the usual psychedelic 70's carpet, old leather couch with a throw on it and a picture of Elvis over the mantelpiece that are 'de rigueur' for the area.

Ken, taking his cap off and sounding sympathetic: "Hello, what's happened?"

Male, sounding devastated: "It's our Mum, she lives here alone and we hadn't heard from her all day and I just had a feeling that something wasn't right so we've come round tonight and she's upstairs in bed. She's gone."

Ken, again sympathetic: "I'm very sorry to hear that. Did she have any history of illness?"

The female pipes up: "She's had a heart problem for years."

Ken, oozing sympathy and professionalism: "Ah. Look, I'm sorry to ask this but can one of you come upstairs and identify her to me? I don't want to put you through too much. We'll just go into the room and if you just nod to me, I'll take that as an official identification."

Male, reluctantly: "I'll do it."

Ken and the male go up a really steep set of stairs and into the front bedroom.

The deceased is propped up in bed, eyes open and staring blankly, obviously dead.

She's a big woman, looking to be about 20 stone in weight.

Ken goes over and tries to take her pulse under her neck, then takes his hand away and looks to the male who nods solemnly, tears filling his eyes.

Ken, consolingly: "That's good mate, well done. I'm sorry but I have to check her over to make sure that there's been no foul play. You don't want to see that. Why don't you go down stairs and ask my colleague to come up?"

The male leaves and Ken waits until Dan enters the room.

Dan (in a quiet voice): "Fucking hell, mate, why've you asked me up? I told you I hate this kind of thing."

Ken (quietly): "Look at the fucking size of her mate. I need to roll her over and check there's no dodgy injuries or we'll get in the shit. I can't shift her on my own."

Ken and Dan both roll her over and check her back, Dan is looking really pale throughout and retching silently.

They lower her back down, Dan getting as far away from the body as quickly as he can but still retching.

Ken: "Delta Mike 1 1."

Radio: "Delta Mike 1 1. Go ahead."

Ken: "Yeah, reference this job in West End Street. Can we have the on call doctor out to pronounce death and can you start the ball rolling with the undertakers to transport to the mortuary."

Radio: "Will Do."

Ken and Dan leave the room and go downstairs.

0110 hrs.

The doctor and the undertakers have arrived. The doctor comes down stairs where Ken, Dan, the male, female and 2 sombrely dressed men, the undertakers, are waiting.

Doctor: "I can confirm certified at 0110hrs."

Ken, "Thank you, Doctor."

As the doctor leaves, one of the undertakers nods his head to Ken indicating he wants to speak to him outside.

Ken complies.

Undertaker, speaking quietly so the relatives can't hear: "I wouldn't normally ask this, mate, but can you and your oppo give us a hand getting her down the stairs, she's a big un and the stairs are steep. Also, it might be best if the relatives aren't here for it."

Ken: "Yeah, no problem. My oppo will be made up."

They re-enter the house.

Ken speaks to the relatives. "I'm sorry to ask this but is there anywhere you can go for a few minutes while we bring her down stairs? It might not be the most pleasant thing to see so probably best if you aren't here for it."

Female, sounding thankful: "I live at No 33, we'll go there."

Ken, nodding his head: "Probably best, I'll come and give you a knock when she's on her way to the mortuary."

The male and female leave the house and Dan, Ken and the 2 undertakers head into the front bedroom.

Dan keeps out of it while Ken and the other 2 struggle as they place the body in a clear bag and then into a large black zipper bag.

They then start to lift her, Dan to the left foot end, Ken the right foot end and the 2 undertakers at the top. They struggle, all sweating, to move the bag down the steep stairs.

As they get to the bottom, there's a sharp turn into the living room and Ken has just stepped off the last step whilst Dan is against the wall at the bottom of the stairs.

At this point, the undertakers lose control and the bag falls forward but because they are still trying to keep hold, the black bag opens and the body starts to come out, ending up cheek to cheek with Dan who is stuck pinned against the wall.

Dan, with real panic and desperation in his voice: "Aargh! Get her off me, get her off me!"

Ken and the undertakers stand still in shock for a second then lose control, all starting to giggle and laugh.

Dan, getting more and more panicked: "Stop fucking laughing and get her off me! I'm going to be sick!"

They regain control of themselves and start to pull the bag off Dan, still giggling every now and then.

Once she is off, Dan can't get into the kitchen quickly enough and starts being sick in the sink.

Undertaker 1, still chuckling: "Looked like he'd bagged off there."

Undertaker 2, having to comment: "Yeah, thought he was going to slip the tongue in."

0130hrs.

In a local scrap yard, Johnny and Stevo, 2 local criminals, dressed in dark clothing, are mooching around to see if there is anything they can steal when a Police car pulls into the car park and up to the barrier that blocks entry into the yard; its headlights sweep across the location.

In the patrol car are Carol and Neil. Carol is a white female in her late twenties, 5ft 4in tall and thin build, brunette hair up in a bun. She has been in the Police for 12 years. Transferring to St.Helens 6 months ago, she is the only 'scouser' on the section. Neil is a good looking white male in his mid-thirties, tanned, short dark hair in a side parting and 6ft 2in tall. He has been in the Police for 10 years, initially joining the Met but transferring to Merseyside after 3 years in the job.

Johnny and Stevo throw themselves to the floor.

Johnny hisses: "Shit, it's the bizzies!"

They flatten themselves to the floor as the patrol car lights are turned off, Stevo, muttering to himself: "Shit, Shit, Shit, Shit, Shit!"

They wait there for a little bit but no one gets out of the vehicle.

Stevo, puzzled, whispers: "What's going on? Why haven't they got out?"

Johnny, the decisive one of the pair: "We can't stay here forever mate, we'll have to risk getting past them. Maybe they've pulled in for a quick kip."

They start to move 'commando style' across the yard, slithering through the muddy enclosure towards the gate.

As they crawl under the barrier and closer to the car they can see Neil in DM 2 1 sat upright in the driver's seat, his eyes closed.

Johnny can't resist and pops his head up at the passenger window and sees Carol with her head in Neil's lap, bobbing up and down.

Johnny grins, turns to Stevo and makes a gesture, one hand clenched going towards one cheek of his face and using his tongue to push the opposite cheek in and out.

Stevo pops his head up for look and also grins and then they drop down and creep away from the entrance.

When they are clear, they stand up and walk away down the street, chatting.

Johnny: "That was that copper Neil, bad lad him, always shagging."

Stevo, laughing:"Yeah, I heard he did your sister."

Johnny, also laughing:"Tosser, it was your Ma."

Stevo: "Tosser."

Johnny: "Who was that with him?"

Stevo: "How do I know, ya blurt? I could only see the back of her head."

As they continue walking further down the road another Police car pulls up next to them. It's Dan and Ken.

Dan, all jovial: "It's Johnny and Stevo! Up to no good lads, you're covered in shite?"

Johnny, respectfully: "Not us boss, innocent as the day is long us."

Stevo, getting his distraction in quickly: "Not like your mate, that bizzie Neil, he's getting a blowie in the scrap yard."

Johnny, nodding: "Top shagger him, boss."

Dan and Ken can hardly contain their excitement.

Ken, almost tripping over his own words: "Right. On your way lads. If we see you about again tonight, we'll be turning you over."

Dan and Ken drive down to just before the scrap yard and park up. They get out as quietly as they can, gently closing the doors rather than slamming them shut.

Dan has his mobile phone out at the ready.

They creep into the yard and up to the Police car.

Dan takes a photo at the driver's side and then another as Carol's head pops up.

They both then run back to their car.

Neil jumps out of his car trying to do his pants up and runs after them, shouting:"You bastards! I'll have you for this!"

Once in the car, Dan shows Ken the photos – one of the back of Carol's head in Neil's lap and then another of her shocked face, looking up at the Police car window.

Ken, laughs. "Brilliant that mate! Now delete it."

Dan: "Eh? What for?"

Ken: "It's alright as a wind up but stuff like that stays between the section. You don't want that on your phone if the rubber heels squad from Professional Standards come knocking on your door."

Dan, the penny dropping: "Ah, got ya."

0200hrs.

Ken and Dan are on patrol when they spot a small rubbish fire on a field. Ken spins the car around and drives onto the field.

Ken, "We'll have to call that in and get the Fire Service out."

Dan, puzzled, "What? It's only a tiddly little thing, it'll burn itself out."

Ken, "Have you learnt nothing from me in the last couple of years?"

Dan, "What do you mean?"

Ken, "Always call the Fire Service out on nights."

Dan, "Eh?"

Ken, the font of all knowledge: "If you don't, the water wasters just get paid for sleeping all night, the lazy bastards. Then they're all fresh for their second jobs during the day. I honestly believe they should get a reduced rate of pay if they go in and get to sleep all night when we run around like blue arsed flies all night."

Then, into his radio: "Delta Mike 1 1 to control."

Radio, "Go ahead, Delta Mike 1 1."

Ken, "Yeah, thanks can we have the fire service out to a rubbish fire on the fields Newton Rd please?"

Radio: "Yeah Roger that, I'll contact them now."

Ken: "Many Thanks."

0215hrs.

A Fire Engine pulls up at the scene. The crew inside are looking all bleary eyed having been woken from their slumber to turn out.

Fire Officer 1, in disbelief: "Is that it? Why the bleeding hell have they called us out to this?"

Fire Officer 2: "Look! It's that wanker Ken, he's called us out on purpose to get us out of bed, the tosser."

The crew start to get out of the Fire Engine and the Lead Fire Fighter approaches Ken.

Lead Firefighter: "Why have you called us to this, Officer? A small fire like that in this location will just burn itself out."

Ken, all innocence: "Ah, will it? Sorry, but I'm no expert in fires, that's what you guys are for. Better safe than sorry, eh?"

The Lead Firefighter looks exasperated but knows there is nothing else he can say so he turns back to start organising the crew.

Firefighter 2 walks past Ken carrying the hose. "You're a Dickhead Ken."

Ken can't resist. "What's up, Princess, did I disturb your beauty sleep? We'll leave it with you."

Ken and Dan walk back towards the Police Car and get in.

Ken, with real glee in his voice: "I'm buzzing now, love sticking one up to the water wasters."

0245hrs.

Back at the station, Dan and Ken have just brought a brew down for Zarah who is covering the Front Office for Chris while he has his refreshments break. Zarah is a really attractive Asian female in her mid-twenties, 5ft 5in tall and quite an athletic build, jet black hair up in a bun. Zarah has been in the Police for about 5 years, coming to the block just before Dan.

Zarah: "Don't you 2 think you'll be getting me with the same prank you got Chris with before. He's told me all about it."

Ken: "Wouldn't dream of doing that to you, Zarah."

Zarah: "Yeah right, forgive me if I check."

At this she gets on her hands and knees to look under the office chair, her back towards them.

Ken's eyes enlarge as he looks at her bottom. He starts nodding vigorously towards Dan who also looks and makes a whistling type face at him. As Zarah gets back up and turns to face them they immediately assume passive faces.

Ken: "See, told you."

Zarah, still suspicious: "Hmm, you're up to something though, you 2 always are."

Dan, "Not us, Zarah. We'll see you later."

Dan and Ken then walk off down the corridor and soon they are out of earshot.

Dan: "Bloody hell, mate, did you see that? How tight were her pants?"

Ken: "Tell me about it. She must go to stores to try on her uniform pants and say to the staff there, ' They're a perfect fit, I'll take a size smaller'."

They have now ended up outside the ladies toilets.

Ken: "Keep a lookout for me mate, just going to set something up."

He enters the toilets and takes a roll of cling film from inside his jacket, enters a cubicle and places it across the toilet bowl then puts the seat back down.

Leaving the toilets, Ken: "Sorted mate, that'll get someone later."

Dan: "Cling film trick?"

Ken: "Yep."

Dan: "Classic."

0255hrs.

In the Front Office at the station, Chris has just come back to take over the duties.

Zarah: "Those 2 buggers were down here before, thought they were going to do that chair thing on me. Thanks for the warning."

Chris: "No worries. They'll be up to something though. Those two always are."

Zarah then makes her way to the ladies toilets. She enters the cubicle and turns around. Undoing her pants, she pulls them down, sits on the toilet and starts to go.

She immediately jumps up with a scream.

Zarah: "The pair of bastards. I knew they'd do something."

0300hrs.

In the refreshments room, Zarah is sat eating her sandwiches when Ken and Dan walk in.

Zarah: "Which one of you numptys put the cling film on the bog?"

Ken: "Not us, Zarah."

Zarah: "Yeah right."

Ken empties his pockets and sits down.

He puts a cricket box on the table in front of him.

Zarah: "What's that?"

Ken: "What this? Got it at Officer Safety Training last week. You know how they've always said that CS only affects the prisoner and not you but we've all found different?"

Zarah: "Yeah?"

Ken? "Well, they're trialling this to hold over your nose and mouth for when you've used CS or have to go into a room when it's been used. Don't think it'll catch on myself."

Zarah: "Let's have a look then."

Ken hands it to Zarah.

Ken: "That's it, the narrow bit goes over your nose and the broad bit over your mouth and chin. Now try and breathe deeply through it."

Zarah follows his instructions and takes deep breaths in and out with the cricket box on her face.

At this point Sgt Brodie enters the room and stops dead in his tracks.

Sgt Brodie is in his late forties, 6ft tall, thin build with dark hair swept back over his head, heavily gelled. He has been in the Police for 20 years, getting promoted quite early but never progressing beyond Sgt.

Sgt Brodie: "What the bleeding hell are you doing there with a groin protector on your face?"

Zarah immediately takes the cricket box off her face and throws it at Ken.

Zarah: "Urghh, you dirty bastard."

Ken, laughing: "You've smelled my balls. Only messing Zarah, it's a new one."

He picks up the cricket box and puts it in his pocket then sits down next to Dan, who has happily sat through all this munching away at the biggest donner kebab you've ever seen.

Ken: "I don't know how you can eat one of those unless you've had a drink."

Dan, in between munching: "Love them, granted they are better after a few beers when they turn into a 'magic' kebab."

Ken: "What are you on about?"

Dan: "It's when you're pissed up and get one of these and you can't get a taxi so you decide to walk home. You trudge away scoffing it and no matter how far you've got to go, just as you finish it and look up, you're at the end of your street. It's magic!"

Ken: "You're a knobhead."

Sgt Brodie: "Are you not eating, Ken?"

Ken: "Nah, Sarge. This shift work messes with my insides. Might try and grab something 'on the hoof' later."

Sgt Brodie: "I know what you mean. Working 3 shifts for a period of time messes with your body, big time."

Ken: "I was reading somewhere that if you do it for a prolonged period it can take years off your life."

Sgt Brodie: "Yeah, I think I've read that somewhere myself. No wonder so many of us drop dead a couple of years after retiring."

They ponder this in silence for a little bit.

Ken: "Yep TJF - The Jobs Fucked. Does you over even when you've done your 30 years."

Sgt Brodie: "Tell you what though, it's always good when you see those notifications in Force Orders of a retired bobby who has passed

21

away at 90 odd years of age. I always think, well in my son, made the bastards pay out plenty of pension there."

Ken: "I know what you mean, be nicer to see a lot more of them though."

0405hrs.

Dan and Ken are on Patrol.

Ken: "Fucking Hell mate, funniest thing I've ever seen at that sudden puddin, her face pressed against yours, last time I saw you that scared was when you had to get a round in."

Dan: "Piss off, you wanker. Told you I don't like bodies. I might be going off with stress tomorrow."

Radio: "Delta Mike 1 1."

Dan: "Delta Mike 1 1. Go Ahead."

Radio: "Thanks. Can you make to an IR IR please? Violent Domestic in progress. No 5 Parr Stocks Crescent."

Dan: "Roger. Will Do."

Ken: "Think B Block went there last week, said the bloke was a real handful."

Dan: "Just our bloody luck that."

Ken turns on the blue light and sirens and starts driving to the job.

0410hrs.

They arrive at scene, it's quite a rundown area, the kind of houses that the council threw up 10 years ago and nobody has bothered to look after since. On the path outside No.5 is a large muscular male just in a pair of tracksuit pants -the kind of bloke who doesn't appear to have a neck and walks around with imaginary carpets under his arms.

Dan: "Fuck me, he's a big bastard."

They get out of the Police car and start to approach him.

Male: "You 2 can fuck off as well!"

Dan: "Easy does it, matey, what's going on?"

Male: "Our Maud has locked me out but it's got fuck all to do with you, so fuck off."

Dan: "Now mate, you know if we get called out we've got to come."

Male: "I don't give a flying fuck! Now do one or you'll both get a good hiding like that bitch is gonna get when I get inside."

At this stage he starts to perform 'karate style' kicks and punches into the fresh air.

Ken and Dan look at each other a bit concerned.

Ken: "Delta Mike 1 1 to Control?"

Radio: "Delta Mike 1 1 go ahead."

Ken:, "Yeah thanks, could we have some back up Parr Stocks Crescent please. This fella is a bit of a unit and looks to be a bit of a handful."

Radio: "Roger, any patrols available please to back up Delta Mike 1 1 at No 5 Parr Stocks Crescent? Violent Domestic."

Over the radio: "Delta Mike 1 2 nearby and making."

Radio: "Delta Mike 1 2 making, thank you."

Ken and Dan look at each other relieved and grin.

In Delta Mike 1 2 is Rob. Rob is known as a bit of a hard man on the block. He's 40 years old, a black male, 5ft 10in tall and stocky build, shaved head and a goatee beard. He served in the military before joining the police 10 years ago. The Block know he was in the Paratroopers at one stage but he doesn't talk about what else he's done which leads them to think he may have been Special Forces at some stage but, like most of those who genuinely have been, he doesn't brag about it.

The male is still 'shadow fighting'. "Come on then, let's have yer! I'll kick the shit out of the pair of you."

Dan: "Now then, mate, we don't want to fight you. I can see you're a handy lad, but this fella turning up next loves a good scrap, he'll take you on."

Male: "Who is it? I'll kick the crap out of him. All you bizzies can't fight for shit."

Ken: "Alright mate, just take it easy, he won't be long. It's a lad called Rob, he handles all my personal confrontations."

Male: "I've heard of him, thinks he's hard doesn't he?"

Dan: "Ex Para mate, and we think some other stuff to but he won't talk about it."

Male: "Bullshit, I'm gonna knock seven kinds of shit out of him when he gets here and then you can all fuck off while I get in and put her in her place."

Blue lights are approaching and Rob arrives in Delta Mike 1 2 and gets out of the Police car.

The male squares up for a second.

Male: "Come on then! I'm gonna rip your fucking head off!"

He then starts to do stretches, kicks and shadow boxing as Rob walks down the path.

As he stands up from a stretch, Rob steps in and punches him in the nose, the sound of it shattering plain for everyone to hear, and then it starts pouring with blood. The male drops to his knees, holding his face and crying: "I wasn't ready!"

Rob: "All yours boys, sorted."

He walks to his car, gets in and drives off.

Dan walks behind the male grabs his arms and handcuffs him to the rear.

Dan and Ken, giggling, walk their prisoner to the car.

Ken, to the male: "That worked out well for you didn't it?"

Dan: "That matey, was what is called a pre-emptive strike."

They place him inside their vehicle, on the rear passenger side, and Dan gets in next to him behind the driver's seat.

Ken into his radio: "Delta Mike 1 1 to control."

Radio: "Go ahead Delta Mike 1 1."

Ken: "Yeah thanks, can St.Helens accept one adult male for a Breach of the Peace please."

Radio: "Standby, I'll check for you."

Ken gets in the driver's seat and they drive off heading towards St.Helens Police station.

0450hrs.

Zarah is on patrol.

As she drives down the road, she spots another police car parked up on a garage forecourt and waves. There is no response from the occupant.

26

Zarah thinks: "That was definitely Ted. Why didn't he wave back?"

Ted is 52 years old, slim build, 6ft tall with short grey hair and a grey moustache. He's been in the Police for over 29 years and is seeing out his time until retirement.

She turns the car around and she has another slow drive past.

Zarah: "Yep defo asleep, mouth wide open, catching flies."

She goes a little further down the road, parks up and gets her phone out.

Zarah, into her phone: "Ken, are you anywhere near Chamberlain Street?"

Pause.

Zarah: "I've found Ted having a kip, dead to the world."

Pause.

Zarah: "Yeah, see you in five."

She puts her phone away and relaxes back into the seat, grinning.

0500hrs.

Ken and Dan arrive and get out of the vehicle and meet up with Zarah.

Ken: "He's fast asleep?"

Zarah: "Yep, well gone."

Ken: "Should we do the torch trick?"

Dan: "That'll wake the old bugger up."

All 3 of them creep up to where Ted is asleep and shine their torches under their chins and start banging on the windows of the car, yelling wildly.

Ted wakes up with a scream.

When he eventually calms down a little, he says: "Was that your idea, Ken?"

Ken: "Did it make you do one of those shitty farts?"

Ted: "Luckily, I didn't have a shart but you very nearly gave me a bloody heart attack. You'll get your comeuppance one day."

0545hrs.

Dan & Ken are in the all night café. It's the kind of greasy spoon place that you can catch salmonella in, just by driving past too slowly.

Dan: "Fucking starving, me lad."

Ken: "You've only just had the biggest kebab I've ever seen."

Dan: "What can I say, like me food me. I'll pay tonight. Fry Up?"

Ken: "Go on then, think I can manage a little something?"

A waitress approaches the table. She doesn't look the cleanest person you've ever seen, stains on her uniform and visible sweat marks in the armpit areas.

Dan: "Ay up, flower. 2 Mega Breakfasts please and 2 large coffees."

The waitress returns to the counter.

Dan: "Wonder if Neil's done in Carol yet?"

Ken: "Probably, he's shagged just about every straight woman in the Force."

Dan: "Lucky bastard, married and still putting it about like that. Here's me single and can't get a sniff."

Ken: "Have you seen the knob on him though? Hung like a Himalayan Yak! It's like a baby's arm with an orange in its hand. No wonder all the birds call him Tripod. I swear when he shakes it in the urinal, it bangs on the sides."

Ken emphasises this by banging on the table.

Dan looks down at his belly. "Lucky Bastard, don't think I've seen mine for years. Shame about Carol, nice girl, she'll be walking like she's got off John Wayne's horse later. Still, she's not as nice as Zarah, body on her is amazing."

Ken: "You're better off steering clear anyway. I got told early on it's the 3 P's that can get you in the shit. Pocket Notebooks, Property and Police partners. That last one rarely works out."

The waitress brings over the large plates and sets them down.

On each plate are 4 rashers of bacon, 4 sausages, 2 Black Puddings, 4 Hash Browns, 3 fried eggs, a pile of fried mushrooms and some baked beans.

They both look down at the plates, Dan licking his lips, Ken in disbelief.

Dan: "You thinking what I'm thinking?"

Thinking that it's way too much Ken, sighs: "Erm, yeah."

Dan holds his hand up to the waitress with 2 fingers extended.

Dan: "2 rounds of toast each please, love."

Dan and Ken are tucking into their meals and it's truly a fascinating experience to watch Dan eat, lots of slurps and moans of enjoyment.

The waitress approaches the table with 2 large cups of coffee and places them down.

Waitress: "2 coffees, oh and here's your toast." She lifts her arm and the pieces of toast fall to the table from her armpit area.

Ken looks horrified, but Dan just scoops them up and puts them to the side of his plate then happily dips a piece into one of his egg yolks.

Dan: "What was that old bugger Ted off with last week?"

Ken: "Stress I think."

Dan: "What? Again? Fucking headworker."

Ken: "Bloody hell, mate, he's got 29 years in on the Job, all of it on the streets. Give him a break, it messes your head up."

Dan: "Don't be daft, it's a buzz."

Ken: "How long have you got in now? 5 years?"

Dan: "Yep, loved every minute."

Ken: "Give it time, it catches up on you. I don't know of anyone who has left the Job without some mental scars. I was reading somewhere that the average person deals with 2 or 3 traumatic experiences in their lifetime and the average cop deals with between 400 and 600. It adds up mate."

Dan:"Nah, he's working the head."

Ken:"I don't begrudge him the odd day off to get his head as straight as he can. Twelve months to do and if he's got mental problems when he retires the Job couldn't care less. Once you're gone, you're gone and the Job couldn't give a toss about you then, drop you like a stone. If you get mental health problems when you're still in, people start treating you like a leper and the job just offers you 6 counselling sessions. Fucking 6, you've hardly had time to remember the counsellor's name."

Dan has by now finished his meal and in between talking and listening to Ken whilst watching Ken's plate like a cat watching a mouse because he can see Ken is struggling.

Dan: "You struggling mate?"

Ken: "Yeah, I've had enough."

Dan reaches across the table and slides Ken's plate towards himself: "Bonus."

Ken, shaking his head: "Kin ell lad, are you ever full?"

Dan, in between chewing: "Full? What's that?"

Ken: "That's all gonna catch up to you eventually."

Dan: "Fucking hell, Ken, you sound like me Mam."

0650hrs.

The Section are in the Sgts Office to go off Duty. The Sgt is signing notebooks. Chris, Rob, Neil, Ted, Zarah and Carol are already there when Dan and Ken enter.

Dan has food stains on his shirt.

Neil: "Been for your usual, ya fat bastard?"

Dan: "Piss off. The only reason I'm fat is cos whenever I shag your Mrs she makes me a bacon butty."

The Sgt Brodie looks up: "Now, now, calm it down."

32

He takes Carol's notebook which is filled with writing and has to turn to a new page to find room to sign.

Sgt Brodie looks up at her: "Left your notebook unattended tonight, Carol?"

He show's the new page in her notebook that contains a huge drawing of a dick and big hairy balls.

Carol: "Bastards!"

The Inspector has actually bothered to come out of his office to see the staff going off duty.

Inspector Bradley is even more overweight than Dan with a huge belly sticking out in front of him. He is 6ft tall, a white male, short grey hair in a flat top which looks a bit ridiculous as his face is wider than his hairstyle. He is 40 years old and has been in the Police for 17 years.

Inspector Bradley to Ken and Dan: "Where have you 2 been?"

Ken: "We've been dealing with that job, Boss."

The rest of the Section zero in as they know there haven't been any jobs given out for the last hour or so.

Inspector Bradley: "What job?"

Ken: "You mean the radio room didn't tell you?"

Inspector Bradley: "No, What job?"

Ken: "I can't understand that, I asked them to tell you."

Inspector Bradley: "They didn't. What job?"

Ken: "At The Elephant Pub in Thatto Heath."

Inspector Bradley: "What's happened there?"

Ken: "Bad one really."

Inspector Bradley: "What?"

Ken: "It was the landlord wasn't it."

Inspector Bradley: "What's he done?"

Ken: "Well, he's had one of the barmaids tied up in the cellar since closing time."

Inspector Bradley: "What! Unlawful imprisonment?"

Ken: "Yeah, but that's not the worst of it."

Inspector Bradley: "Why, what else?"

Ken: "He's had her tied to a chair naked."

Inspector Bradley: "Really?"

Ken: "Yeah and it gets worse."

Inspector Bradley: "What else?"

Ken: "I can't believe the radio room didn't make you aware."

The Inspector is well and truly hooked, now hanging on Ken's every word, leaning in to get more information.

Inspector Bradley: "They didn't. What else happened?"

Ken: "Well, with her being tied up." He pauses.

Inspector Bradley: "Yes?"

Ken: "And naked and all that." He pauses again.

Inspector Bradley: "Yes?"

Ken: "He's been performing oral sex on her for hours."

Inspector Bradley: "What? Really? The pervert! I hope you've got him in the cells."

Ken: "Well, we were going to, boss, but we had to let him go."

Inspector Bradley, outraged: "What do you mean you had to let him go!"

Ken: "Well, it turns out that he wasn't breaking any laws was he?"

Inspector Bradley: "What do you mean he wasn't breaking any laws?"

Ken: "Well, we checked and everything but." He pauses.

Inspector Bradley: "What?"

Ken: "Well he's got a licker license hasn't he?"

The Section burst out laughing. Inspector Bradley is incensed though, his face turning a funny shade of purple but, before he can say anything, Sgt Brodie jumps to his feet and declares: "Right you lot, get yourselves off and we'll see you next shift."

Second Nightshift.

Friday.

2200hrs.

The Section are in the Parade Room all sat around a table as Sgt Brodie is about to read out the duties for the night.

Radio: "All Patrols, we have a Con Requires assistance outside The Plaza in Duke Street."

Rob: "Carrier, Sarge?"

Sgt Brodie: "Let's go."

Rob jumps up and grabs the Carrier keys off a hook on the wall and they all run out of the office.

2215hrs.

In the Police carrier. The Section are making their way back to the Police Station.

Rob is driving with Sgt Brodie in the front seat. In the back, the rest of the Section are in the seats and there is also a Prisoner in the cage at the back.

Sgt Brodie: "Couldn't help yourself could you? You were on that prisoner quicker than a tramp on a butty."

Rob: "Sarge, I'm not having someone kicking off like that and a job's a job. Wonder what started the whole kick off anyway."

Sgt Brodie: "That plonker from the Town Centre Section, Dave Murphy, put the Con Requires out."

Rob: "Sergeant Major Danger? Could start a fight in an empty room that pillock. Best thing you did was approving his transfer from us to them. We were sick of rushing to his assistance and then finding out that he was usually the cause of the problem."

Sgt Brodie: "I bet before he turned up it was a typical NHI job."

Zarah: "NHI?"

Sgt Brodie: "No Humans Involved."

Dan isn't looking too good in the back. His face is pale but he's sweating profusely.

Ken: "What's up with you, lad?"

Dan: "It's that kebab last night mate. I think it was a bit dodgy, my stomach is creasing me."

Dan then lifts one of his cheeks off the seat and lets out a really long, rasping fart. The relief on his face is obvious.

Zarah: "You dirty bastard."

Neil, almost gagging: "Fucking hell that's ripe that is. Rob! Rob! Stop the bus!"

Rob pulls over and they all jump out, wafting their hands in front of their faces.

Ted: "You need raking out, Dan. That was horrendous."

Dan: "You're just jealous cos at your age you can't trust a fart, just in case it ends up as a shart."

Prisoner shouting from inside the Carrier: "Boss! Boss! Let me out, it fucking stinks!" Then there is the sound of wretching as he is sick in the cage.

Sgt Brodie: "You'll be cleaning that up before we go out again, Dan."

2225hrs.

In the Station toilets.

Ken is sat in the cubicle, sweating and trying to go. He strains and then sighs, muttering to himself: "Fuck's sake, come out will you."

There's thudding of rushing feet and the cubicle door next to him crashes open.

Dan: "Shit! Shit! Shit!"

The door slams shut and Dan fumbles with his clothing and then there's the sound of an almighty sloppy crap hitting the bowl.

38

Ken: "Fucking hell, Dan. I wish that was me."

Dan: "So do I mate, I've not got me pants down yet."

Ken laughs.

Dan: "I only just made that. A couple more seconds and it would have been shartmageddon!"

Ken laughs even more and then suddenly stops. "Oh, that's worked."

Silence for a little bit as the lads concentrate on the job in hand.

Dan: "Why's the Sarge split us up tonight mate?"

Ken: "Not sure, mate, said he wanted a chat with you."

Dan: "Wonder what that's about?"

Ken, lying: "No idea, mate."

Ken goes to get some toilet paper off the roll. "Fuck's sake, there's not enough bog roll here. Do me a favour and pass some under, mate."

Dan starts to get some and as he is doing so, Ken, ever prepared to play a prank on someone, gets a small packet of chocolate spread out of his shirt pocket.

Dan: "Here you go."

His hand appears under the partition and Ken begins to take the toilet roll off him but, at the same time, wipes some chocolate spread on Dan's hand.

Ken: "Ta cocker."

Dan: "You dirty bastard! Is that shit?"

Ken bursts out laughing.

Dan: "It is isn't it?"

Ken: "Sniff it and see."

Dan, after a few seconds: "Got me, mate. Good one."

0030hrs.

Neil and Chris are paired up tonight. They've been to a sudden death and have asked for the on call Doctor to pronounce life extinct. They're watching out of the window, waiting for the Doctor to arrive.

Neil: "Still okay dealing with the Doc, mate?"

Chris: "Yeah, then I can put it in my portfolio that I've dealt with a Sudden Pudden."

The Doctor pulls up and starts to get out of his car.

Neil: "Shit, this Doctor's a bit of a stickler mate, likes being called by his full name all the time. Dr Timberdick."

Chris: "Righto, got you."

The Doctor enters the house.

Chris: "Hello, Dr Timberdick, it's just through here."

The Doctor shoots Chris a dirty look but doesn't say anything. He follows Chris to the body and examines it.

Doctor: "Time of death 0032hrs, Officer."

Chris: "Thank you very much, Dr Timberdick."

Neil can hardly contain himself, one of his eyes is even twitching as he tries to stop bursting into laughter.

Doctor: "By the way, officer, my name is Dr Woodcock" then to Neil, "Is this your doing?"

Neil loses it and doubles over spluttering.

The Doctor shakes his head. "I deal with children."

He then walks out of the house.

0100hrs.

Sgt Brodie and Dan are on patrol. Dan is driving.

Sgt Brodie: "So Dan, you've got 5 years in now. What are your plans for the future?"

Dan: "I was thinking of giving Traffic a go, Sarge."

Sgt Brodie: "Well you've got the build for it lad, either that or a Detective."

Dan: "Bloody 'ell, Sarge, that's a bit harsh."

Sgt Brodie: "Not really, I walked past you and the Inspector at the top of the stairs the other day and it was like being at a Darth Vader Convention. Seriously though, Dan, I'm a bit concerned as you've piled the weight on lately. Rumour has it they're going to introduce a yearly fitness test. If you dip that you could get sacked."

Dan: "Nah Sarge, never gonna happen."

Sgt Brodie: "Them's the new regs that are coming, mate, just don't put yourself in that position."

Dan: "If they go for me I'll just put a Freedom of Information request in won't I? I've got a contact at the Training Centre that's told me that the Chief has said he won't be doing it and there'll be loads of bosses and detectives going to avoid it. They'll be opening a can of worms; the Federation will be all over them."

Sgt Brodie: "The Fed? The toothless tiger? All wind and bluster mate."

Dan: "What do we pay our subscriptions for then?"

Sgt Brodie: "Haha, the travel insurance and other deals. They're not much use for anything else. They can only do so much and the bosses and the Government know it. Until we have the ultimate threat of the right to strike they just make noise that gets ignored."

Dan: "Toothless Tiger, never heard that one before."

Sgt Brodie: "Seriously Dan, if you put your head up above the parapet they'll make your life difficult. There's some vindictive bastards in this job."

Dan: "How do you mean?"

Sgt Brodie: "Where do you live, mate?"

Dan: "Haydock."

Sgt Brodie: "Upset them and they'll move you over to the Wirral or something like that, just to make life difficult. All the notice they've got to give you for a move is 28 days."

Dan: "Bastards."

Sgt Brodie: "Who's your contact at the Training Centre then?"

Dan: "Tim Harris, joined with him."

Sgt Brodie: "Tim? Tim Nice but Dim? I'd take whatever he says with a pinch of salt - thick as a whale omelette that lad. Last time I was on a course there, I was asking the group where I could get some cheap wood to make some garden furniture and he was listening in. He thought Palletland was a theme park."

Dan: "Have you heard the best story about him? He was working overtime on the footy and, because it was cold, the Operational Order had a line in it saying that due to Officer Safety no scarves were to be worn. Half time comes and he walks into the Police Room, arms full of red & white scarves that he'd seized off the supporters."

Sgt Brodie: "I don't mind going to the Training Centre for Officer Safety instruction."

Dan: "Yeah, I dread it every year and then end up enjoying it when I get there."

Sgt Brodie: "Depends on who you get though. There's some there with a real knowledge of the subject who are good trainers and there are some who don't have a clue and just try to be your mate to get good feedback."

Radio: "Patrols, to make a Personal Attack Alarm at the Windle Island Garage on the East Lancs Road."

Sgt Brodie: "Delta Sierra 1 2 making."

Dan puts on the blue lights and sirens and starts to accelerate, concentrating on the twists and turns of the road they are on.

Sgt Brodie: "You'll be putting your head above the parapet if you make waves over the fitness, Dan. Some of these bastards higher up have got long memories."

Dan, looking at Sgt Brodie: "Nah, they'll shit themselves."

As this is happening, there is a sharp bend in the road that Dan has missed because he turned his head.

Sgt Brodie notices and shouts: "Bend!"whilst grabbing the handle above the door.

Dan completely misses it and the car leaves the road, flying into the air then bouncing around as it goes into a ploughed farmer's field,

Sgt Brodie and Dan are being thrown around in the car, screaming.

Sgt Brodie: "Shit, shit, shit!"

Dan: "We're gonna die!"

The car comes to a halt with both of them looking traumatised. Sgt Brodie shoots daggers at Dan who is still tightly gripping the steering wheel. He turns slowly to look at Sgt Brodie.

Dan: "I know a short cut."

Sgt Brodie loses it. "Shortcut! Fucking Shortcut! I nearly shat myself. You're grounded. Front Office for you for the rest of the night."

0130hrs.

Delta Romeo 1 1 - Rob and Ted are on patrol in the immediate response car.

Radio: "All Patrols, observations for a Blue Mondeo part Reg No V326. Been stolen approximately 10 minutes ago from the car park of Rainhill Labour Club."

Rob, in the passenger seat, looks down the road and there is a Mondeo coming in the other direction.

Rob: "This is a Mondeo, could be it."

Ted: "Nah, mate, you never drop on something like that."

Rob: "Fuck me, it is!!! Delta Romeo 1 1 Scramble!! In pursuit of the Mondeo just been circulated as stolen from Rainhill."

Ted spins the Police car around and activates the blue lights and sirens.

Rob: "Vehicle travelling down Prescot Road towards St Helens Town Centre, speeds in excess of 70, seven zero, miles per hour."

Radio: "Delta Romeo 1 1, can you confirm an Advanced Driver is driving?"

Rob: "Confirmed, Advanced Driver. Vehicle now approaching traffic lights, junction with Eccleston Street. Lights are on red, no brakelights and straight through at 70."

Ted is showing all the skills of someone who has been an 'Advanced Police Driver' for many, many years, keeping up with the vehicle but not so close as to cause an accident.

Rob: "Now heading towards the Asda roundabout. On the roundabout, not 1, not 1, not 2, not 2, not 3, not 3, fourth exit on the Linkway, heading towards the traffic lights with Pizza Hut."

Ted effortlessly keeps up the pursuit, calm and composed - smooth gear changes and controlled acceleration. To look at him you'd think he was out for a leisurely Sunday drive.

Rob: "Lights are on red, no brakelights and straight through at 70. Now 80, eight zero, miles per hour heading towards B & Q Roundabout. Brakes, brakes, brakes at the roundabout. Not 1, not 1, second exit on the Linkway towards Tesco Roundabout. Brakes, brakes, brakes! On the roundabout, not 1, not 1, second exit, straight on towards McDonalds Roundabout."

Ted: "Industrial estate coming up, he might be getting ready to bail."

Rob: "Brakes, brakes, brakes at the roundabout, first exit onto Sherdley Road. Brakes, brakes, brakes! It's a left onto Roundwood Drive and he's lost it! Bailing and on foot."

Rob and Ted jump out of the car and Rob starts a bit of cat and mouse around the stolen car with the car thief. Then Ted comes out of nowhere and does a sliding tackle worthy of an Italian defender and takes out the offender.

Ted: "Ow! Me fucking ankle!"

The car thief is on his hands and knees starting to get up when Rob comes barrelling in shouting "Stay down!" and kicks him in the ribs causing him to leave the floor and roll over several times like an Italian striker who's been flicked on the ear. Rob grabs him, puts him into a ground pin position, swiftly applies the handcuffs then picks him up.

Rob: "You thieving bag of shite!"

Ted is standing up and limping.

Rob: "You okay, Ted?"

Ted: "Yeah, Rob. Just a twinge."

Rob: "Delta Romeo 1 1 to Control."

Radio: "Delta Romeo 1 1, go ahead."

Rob: "Thanks Control, one detained suspicion of UTMV, can you see if St Helens will accept please?"

Control Room: "Will do."

A few seconds later – Radio: "Delta Romeo 1 1 from Control."

Rob: "Delta Romeo 1 1 go ahead."

Radio: "Yeah, Delta Romeo 1 1, St Helens will accept your prisoner."

Rob and Ted put the car thief into the back of the Police Car and are about to get in themselves when a plain Fiesta pulls into the road.

A white male in a snazzy suit jumps out and approaches them. It's the Night Duty Detective, Andy Norris.

DC Norris: "Nice catch boys, mind if I jump in the back and have a word with him."

Ted: "What, like a pre PACE interview."

DC Norris: "Now then Ted, no need to be like that."

Ted: "We'll leave it thanks, you can have him back at the Nick."

DC Norris strides off in a huff, jumps into his car and wheel spins away.

Rob: "What was that about mate? Andy Norris is meant to be a great thief taker and a handy lad."

Ted: "Allegedly. The only people I've seen him square up to are kids and drunks. He just wanted to threaten him or make a deal in the car before the interview."

Rob: "Ah, he's one of them."

Ted: "Yeah, 'big rep' and all these young ones hero worship him but most of his jobs are dodgy. I haven't got much time for him and I've got less than a year to do so everything by the book. I'm not losing my pension over a prick like that."

Rob: "Don't blame you mate, steer clear of the likes of him."

Ted: "I will. I call him Just Cause."

Rob: "Don't get you?"

Ted: "Have you never heard of Just Cause Syndrome, mate? It's when a cop is determined to bring someone to justice no matter what they have to do."

Rob: "Ah, ends justify the means type of thing?"

Ted: "Exactly mate, that's him all over."

0150hrs.

Custody Suite. Rob, Ted and their prisoner are in the Doctor's room.

Dr: "And what seems to be the problem?"

The car thief is stood all hunched over to one side.

Car Thief: "It's him isn't it Dr , he's broke me ribs."

He nods his head towards Ted who looks a bit shocked and glances over to Rob who's looking around the room trying to look innocent.

Dr: "And how did this happen?"

Car Thief: "Well Dr, I was in a stolen danny."

Dr: "Danny?"

Car Thief: "Car."

Dr: "Oh right, carry on."

Car Thief: "Well I lost it and then I was trying to get away and that old bizzie kicked me in the ribs."

Dr: "So you crashed a stolen car?"

Car Thief: "Yeah."

Dr: "Right I've seen enough Officers, take him back to the cells."

Rob escorts the prisoner out of the room.

Ted: "What's the verdict Doc?"

Dr: "Nothing to worry about Officer> I'm putting it down as minor injuries consistent with a car crash. Horrible thieving little shitbag."

Ted: "Ah right, nice one Doc."

Dr: "No problem, keep up the Lord's work."

0200hrs.

Neil, Sgt Brodie and Chris are on patrol in the Police Carrier in the Town Centre. They're driving down the road and just coming up to the local lap dancing club, which has just closed.

Outside the club are 3 of the girls, short skirts and crop tops. Neil pulls over in the Carrier.

Neil: "Alright girls, just finished?"

Lapdancer 1: "Hiya, Neil, Yeah, just waiting for a taxi to take us all back to mine but they're saying it'll be an hour."

Neil: "What do you think, Sarge? Can we give the girls a lift home? After all it's q..."

Sgt Brodie: "Don't say it, don't you fucking dare say the Q word or all hell will break loose."

Neil: "Ah righto, what do you think though?"

Sgt Brodie: "Can't do any harm."

Neil: "Go round to the side girls, we'll give you a lift."

The girls open the door and start to get in.

Lapdancer 1: "Oh, look girls, there's a young one hidden in the back."

Chris immediately starts to blush but undeterred Lapdancer 2 sits next to him and swings her legs over his.

Lapdancer 2: "Hello, sweetie. Are you new? What's your name?"

Chris is silent, embarrassed but his eyes are on stalks. They shut the door and drive off.

0210 hrs.

Local new build housing estate.

The carrier pulls up outside a big semi-detached house.

Sgt Brodie: "Dancing pays well then."

Lapdancer 1: "Not bad at all, Sarge. Couple more years and I'll have this paid off."

Neil: "There you go girls, first class service straight to the door."

Lapdancer 1: "Aw Neil, you remembered where I live."

Neil: "Course I did lovely."

Lapdancer 1: "Do you want to come in for a brew?"

Neil: "What do you think, Sarge? Quick brew?"

Sgt Brodie: "Yeah, I'm spitting feathers."

They all troop inside the house and go into the living room. Sgt Brodie is sat on the couch with one of the girls. Chris is in a chair with Lapdancer 2 sat in his lap, still looking nervous and with eyes on stalks. A few minutes later Neil and Lapdancer 1 come into the living room with cups of tea for everyone.

Neil: "Easy there Chris, she won't eat you alive you know."

Lapdancer 2: "Hmm or maybe I will, he's lovely."

Chris looks even more nervous as Neil and Lapdancer 1 go back into the kitchen.

Fifteen minutes later Sgt Brodie is just finishing his brew and looks over at Chris who is still sat in the chair with Lapdancer 2. He's now relaxed and the pair of them are chatting away like old friends.

Sgt Brodie: "Right Chris, we'll have to be going in a minute, not a word of this to anyone son, and I don't want you thinking this is a regular event. Now, where's Neil gone?"

Sgt Brodie stands up and walks into the kitchen where he is greeted by the sight of Neil, pants and underwear down by his ankles but still with his body armour, shirt and flat cap on. He's got Lapdancer 1 bent over the kitchen table and he is going at it hammer and tongs. Neil looks over without even a pause or slowing down.

Neil: "I suppose you want me to stop?"

Sgt Brodie looks at him and shakes his head in disbelief.

Sgt Brodie: "Fuck's sake Neil."

Neil: "Nearly there Sarge, won't be 2 shakes."

Sgt Brodie walks out of the kitchen.

A few minutes later they are in the carrier.

Sgt Brodie: "Feel better for that do you?"

Neil: "Aye, it'll get me through the night that."

Sgt Brodie: "Should have known you had an ulterior motive. You've got a problem you have."

Neil: "She'd been dancing all night though, proper disco fanny. I'll have to have a shower before I go home or the Mrs will smell her on me."

Sgt Brodie shakes his head and turns to Chris.

Sgt Brodie: "Don't be thinking this goes on all the time, and don't be thinking this bloody sex addict is a good role model."

Chris: "Right-o Sarge."

Sgt Brodie: "And wipe your cheek, you've got lipstick on it. Right back to the station for scoff, if we don't show up they'll know something has been going on."

0300hrs.

Ken has just come into the Front Office with a takeaway he's collected for Dan.

Ken: "There you go, Dan. Two large chef's special pizzas and a garlic bread with cheese."

Dan: "Brill mate, I'm famished. I've been waiting that long you can see me ribs."

Ken: "Bloody hell Dan, I think you'd need an ultrasound to see your ribs. Anyway, before your little detour tonight, cakes all round for that tomorrow by the way, what did the Sarge want to speak to you about?"

Dan: "Funny enough it was about my weight, reckons I've piled it on."

Ken: "I'm not being funny mate but he's got a point. You need to cut down on the food and do a bit of exercise. Maybe start going jogging or something."

Dan: "I fucking hate that though, really boring, can't motivate myself."

Ken: "Why don't you ask Zarah, she's a bit of a runner, pounds the pavement regular like. And she was a personal trainer before she joined the job. Maybe she'll take you under her wing."

Dan: "You know something, I think I'll do that."

Any opportunity to spend some time with Zarah sounds like a damned fine idea to Dan.

Dan: "About my accident, fucking Neil was in before gloating and taking the piss."

Ken: "Ignore him mate. He didn't tell one of his 'When I was in the Met' stories did he?"

Dan: "Nah, what's that all about though?

Ken: "Mate, if someone's been in the Met they seem to think they're the elite. They don't realise that all the other Forces in the country look down on them."

Dan: "How do you mean?"

Ken: "Take Neil for example. He went to the Met because he couldn't get in here. Worked a couple of years there and then transferred back here. I know of loads who've done that."

Dan: "I don't get it?"

Ken is on his soapbox again, relishing an opportunity to educate his protégé: "Think about it. The Met can't get enough recruits of a good standard who live within their area, so they open it up for applications around the country. So people who aren't of a good enough standard to get in their own local Force manage to get in the Met. So they're taking on our rejects. Don't get me wrong, they join for the right reasons."

Dan: "Why does he keep bragging about it then?"

Ken: "I think that because they are the biggest Force in the country, they get brainwashed into the old 'biggest is best' rubbish. They've gone for quantity over quality. I've worked on National Operations and Events with them and they're piss poor, mate. Don't even know how to speak to people properly because they don't have to. Put a call for help out and they're inundated with bobbies pretty quick. Whereas here, you can call for help and still be waiting 15 minutes later."

Ken stops and thinks for a minute. "Mind you, to be fair we get that here. Bobbies transfer from the city out to good old sunny St Helens, then realise back up can take a while. Before you've got to know them, they've transferred back within a month."

Dan: "Why can't he see that?"

Ken: "Brainwashed mate, get told it enough times and you believe it. See you upstairs for scoff in a bit."

0415hrs.

Sgt Brodie has jumped in with Ken.

Ken: "How did your chat with Dan go then?"

Sgt Brodie: "Has he spoken to you?"

Ken: "Yeah, he filled me in a bit about you mentioning his weight."

Sgt Brodie: "I like the lad, Ken. He's keen, gets on with job etc but he needs to shift some pounds."

Ken: "Yeah, I backed up what you said, got him thinking a little bit. Hopefully he'll start to do something about it."

Radio: "Any patrol can make a report of a potential jumper on the bridge over the Linkway into Sherdley Park."

Sgt Brodie: "Delta Sierra 1 2 making the last with Delta Mike 1 1."

A few minutes later they arrive at scene and can see a young man has climbed over the railings and is standing looking down at the drop to the road.

Sgt Brodie: "You start talking to him, Ken, and I'll start organising getting the road closed at both ends."

Ken: "Roger that."

Ken approaches the young male, turning his radio off as he does so.

Ken: "Hello mate, what's your name?"

"Darren."

Ken: "Well Darren, my name is Ken, What are you doing?"

Darren: "I'm gonna jump."

Ken: "What makes you want to do that, Darren?"

Darren: "My girlfriend has dumped me and I can't live without her."

Ken: "I'm sorry to hear that Darren. How long were you together?"

Darren: "Two weeks."

Ken is glad that he's stood behind Darren so the lad can't see his face because his expression would just say 'WTAF?'

Meanwhile, Sgt Brodie has arranged for the Linkway to be closed at both ends so that no vehicles come along it.

Inspector Bradley arrives at scene and manages to pull himself out of the car, which immediately raises a few inches.

He blusters up to Sgt Brodie.

Inspector Bradley: "What's the situation Sgt?"

Sgt Brodie: "Young lad threatening to jump, Boss. Ken is talking with him now and I've got the Control room to start the ball rolling for a Negotiator."

Inspector Bradley: "No need for that Sgt. I'm the senior officer on scene and I'll take over now."

Sgt Brodie: "Have you done the Negotiator's course, Boss?"

Inspector Bradley: "No need, I've been told that my negotiating skills are that good that I don't need one. They could learn off me."

At this, he barrels forwards towards Ken and Darren.

Inspector Bradley: "Okay Officer, I'll take over now."

Ken: "We're doing okay, Boss. Me and Darren here are getting along just fine."

Inspector Bradley: "I don't think so. I'm your superior so get over there with Sgt Brodie, that's an order."

Ken reluctantly goes over to Sgt Brodie and whispers

"Who the fuck does he think he is? My Superior? He's my boss, he's not my superior in any way, shape or form. He better not fuck this up."

Inspector Bradley has now approached Darren.

Inspector Bradley: "Now then soft lad, what do you think you are playing at?"

Darren: "I'm gonna jump."

Inspector Bradley: "No you're not. Now stop playing silly beggars and get back over this railing."

Darren: "I will, I'll jump."

Inspector Bradley: "You haven't got the bottle son, this is just a cry for help. You've got our attention, now get back over here."

Darren: "I'll jump, I will."

Inspector Bradley: "Get back over here, I'm a busy man, I've got things to do. Now stop wasting my time."

At this point, Darren let's go of the railing and jumps.

There is silence on top of the bridge for a few seconds and then Darren starts screaming from the road below: "My legs! My legs are broken!"

Inspector Bradley walks over to Sgt Brodie and Ken.

Inspector Bradley: "Well I did my best for him but sometimes these people are just determined to jump. I'll leave you with it, Sgt."

He then walks over to his car and manages to start shoehorning himself in.

Ken turns to the Sarge and just loud enough to be heard says: "Top negotiating skills there. Is he for fucking real?"

Sgt Brodie: "I suppose we'd better get down there and organise a bloodbus to get the poor lad to Hospital."

0645hrs.

Ken is back on his own and having a slow drive in to the Police Station to go off duty.

Radio: "Delta Mike 1 1."

Ken: "Delta Mike 1 1 go ahead."

Radio: "Yeah thanks, could you make The Little Chef on the East Lancs Road please? Report from the manager that there is a male there disturbing the customers."

Ken: "Erm, any chance it can wait for mornings?"

Radio: "Sorry Ken, apparently he's been there for a while and if we wait for mornings it could seven thirty before anyone gets out to them."

Ken: "Yeah Roger, I'll make."

0650hrs.

Ken arrives at the car park of the Little Chef. He gets out of the car and walks into the foyer. There is a male in there sat in a chair, staring blankly into space. Ken goes past him and into main part of the seating area. It is surprisingly busy with the early morning crowd in for a coffee or a breakfast. The Manageress approaches.

Ken: "Hiya, what seems to be the problem?"

Manageress: "Hi, it's that lad in the foyer. A few customers have complained that they feel intimidated by him."

Ken: "Right, okay, has he actually done anything to intimidate them?"

Manageress: "Well, no, not really. He's just been sitting there, muttering to himself every now and again."

Ken: "Well in that case, I don't really have any powers to just throw him out. However, you can ask anyone on the premises to leave and I can be with you to prevent a Breach of the Peace."

Ken and the Manageress go into the foyer.

Manageress: "Hi, I'm the Manager here and I'm asking you to leave as you are frightening the customers."

Ken watches as the male starts to stand up and then, worryingly, continues to stand up to about 6ft 10in tall. He looks at Ken and Ken

63

can see that his pupils are blown wide open and he has a little white foam at the corners of his mouth. Ken gets that premonition type feeling as he just knows what is going to happen next. He just has time to think 'Oh for fuck's sake' as the male launches at him and they crash through the doors into the main seating area.

Ken just has time to shout into his radio: "Delta Mike 1 1 Con Requires."

Ken and the male are engaged in grappling with each other, banging into chairs and tables, a couple of which smash as they collide into them. At one point, Ken lands on his back on a table with the male on top of him. Ken looks over to his right and notices 2 big rugby player types sat at a nearby table sipping their coffees and watching the entertainment with interest. Bizarrely, Ken finds himself calmly thinking to himself 'You just sit there lads, don't bother yourselves enough to come over and give me a hand like'.

Somehow, Ken manages to get the male to the floor and get the handcuffs on him but not in any recognised fashion. The male has ended up with his right hand up and over his head and the left hand up his back. He almost looks as though he has been doing the 'Bring me

Sunshine' dance from the old Morecombe and Wise shows. Ken holds him down and takes a few deep breaths: "Delta Mike 1 1."

Control, "Delta Mike 1 1 go ahead."

Ken: "Thanks, cancel patrols please, male has been detained. Just need a caged vehicle for transport please."

Ken gets the male onto his feet and escorts him outside and starts to reflect upon the 2 lads who just watched him struggling and starts to get angrier and angrier.

By the time Neil and Chris turn up in the carrier he has internally worked himself up into quite a state. As they are putting the male into the cage, Insp Bradley screeches into the car park, jumps out of the car and comes over to Ken.

Inspector Bradley: "What's happened?"

Ken can't contain it anymore and shouts, "What's happened? What's happened? He fucking well kicked off on me, that's what's happened!"

Inspector Bradley, not one for confrontations, takes a couple of steps back and then scurries back to his car.

Inspector Bradley: "Right, right, I'll see you back at the station then."

Neil: "Bloody hell, Ken. Are you okay?"

Ken: "Yeah mate, just leave it, I'll follow you to the Nick"

Third Nightshift.

Saturday

2205hrs.

In the Station.

Dan is sneaking into the female toilets with a cup of water. Once inside, he breaks s ginger biscuit into it and waits until it's all soggy. He then smears it all over the mirror and leaves the toilets.

2210hrs.

Carol goes into the toilets and then,

Carol: "The dirty bastards!"

She comes out into the corridor and bumps into Dan who is trying to look as though he's just nonchalantly walking past.

Carol: "It's disgusting!"

Dan: "What's up Carol?"

Carol: "Some dirty cow has smeared shit all over the mirror in there."

Dan: "You're joking? Let's see."

They both go into the toilets.

Carol: "See, look at the state of that."

Dan licks his finger and runs it across the mirror and then puts it in his mouth.

Dan: "You're right, it's shit."

Carol starts to wretch and runs into a cubicle to be sick.

Dan exits laughing.

2230hrs.

Neil and Chris are paired up again and having a drive around the Town Centre.

Just then they see a male collapsed on the floor and a woman frantically waving them down.

They pull up and get out of the car.

Neil: "What's going on?"

Woman: "We've been out for a meal and he just collapsed about 10 minutes ago. I've called an Ambulance."

Chris, meanwhile, has been checking the male over and shouts to Neil: "Not breathing and no pulse."

He then immediately starts CPR.

Neil, into his radio: "Delta Mike 2 1 to Control."

Radio: "Delta Mike 2 1 go ahead."

Neil: "Can you check with Ambo please, see if they've had a call about a male collapsed in Bridge Street? We're at scene now, no pulse and not breathing. Colleague has started CPR."

Radio: "Roger, stand by."

Neil goes over to Chris and starts to assist with CPR.

Radio: "Delta Mike 2 1."

Neil: "Go ahead,"

Radio: "Ambo on route, ETA 10 minutes."

Neil and Chris work on the male for 10 minutes, swapping roles every now and again from breaths to compressions. By the time the Ambulance turns up they are nearly exhausted.

2245hrs.

The Ambulance has arrived and one of the crew is talking to the female while the other gets the stretcher out of the Ambulance. Then between the 4 of them they get the male onto the stretcher and into the Ambulance.

Paramedic 1 to Chris: "Can you help us in the back mate."

Chris jumps in the back and shuts the doors. Neil stays with the female who is now hysterical.

Inside the Ambulance. Paramedic 1: "Just help us to rock the Ambo a bit mate and follow our lead."

They start to rock the Ambulance but don't touch the male.

Chris is puzzled: "What's going on?"

Paramedic 2: "Mate, great effort out there but he'd popped his clogs well before you even turned up. This is just about making his Mrs think we've tried so she feels better. Stop rocking."

Paramedic 1 shouts: "Clear!"

Then a few seconds later they start rocking the Ambulance again. This goes on for about 10 minutes and then they open the doors and approach the female.

Paramedic 1: "I'm sorry, we couldn't get him back. Do you want to come in the Ambulance with us?"

Paramedic 2: "Thanks for the help lads, you can leave this with us now."

Chris and Neil get back into the Police Car. Chris looks traumatised.

Neil: "What's up mate?"

Chris: "They did nothing, just pretended."

Neil: "Ah, right. They know what they're about, mate. Don't get too down about it. Could have been worse though."

Chris: "How so?"

Neil: "Imagine if St John's Ambulance had turned up."

Chris: "I don't get you."

Neil: "They'd have turned up dragging their back leg and looking at you with a lazy eye. I swear if I was on a stretcher, and they turned up, it'd be an instant cure."

2315hrs.

Carol and Zarah are on patrol.

Zarah: "I hear you had a bit of a dalliance with Neil."

Carol: "Sort of, yeah."

Zarah: "Is it true what they all say about him? He's a big lad?"

Carol: "Yeah, it's true. I've never seen a cock that big."

Zarah: "Did you shag him?"

Carol: "Christ no! It'd split me in two. I gave him a blowjob and that nearly dislocated my jaw. Why? Are you interested in him?"

Zarah: "God no! I like Dan anyway."

Carol, incredulous: "Dan? Dan? As in Dan the Salad Dodger?"

Zarah: "Don't be like that, I know he's put a bit on but I've always liked him."

Carol: "Bloody hell, Zarah. From what I hear half the Nick have been trying to get into your pants for the last 5 years and all this time you've been pining over Mr Blobby."

Zarah: "Don't call him that and don't tell him either."

Just then a big 4 x 4 comes the other way, driving erratically and swerving all over the road.

Zarah: "State of him, we'll have to pull him over."

They turn around and catch up to the vehicle, put the blue lights on and then flash the headlights for the vehicle to stop.

The vehicle stops and they get out and approach it.

Carol: "Turn your engine off and hand me the keys please."

Driver: "Alright love, no problem."

He hands her the keys with a big smile, trying to appear charming, the effect only spoiled by the white powder all over his nose and the strong smell of alcohol coming from him.

Carol: "Okay, we've stopped you because of the way you were driving and now I've spoken to you, you smell strongly of intoxicants. I'm going to require you to provide me with a specimen of breath."

Driver: "Don't be daft love, I'm not doing that. Now be a good girl and give me my keys back."

Carol: "Okay, you are now under arrest for failing to provide a specimen of breath. You do not have to say anything but it may harm your defence if you do not mention when questioned something which you later rely on in court. Anything you do say may be used in evidence."

Driver: "You're wasting your time love, I'll be on my way soon."

Carol draws away from the vehicle a little and speaks to Zarah.

Carol: "He's a big fella."

Zarah: "Isn't that Johnny Bingham? Used to play for the local Rugby team?"

Carol: "Ah, that's where I know his face from. He's meant to be a bit of a prick isn't he ? Should we see if there's anyone nearby to assist?"

Zarah: "Yeah, Rob would be handy around now."

Carol: "Delta Mike 1 2 to Control.

Radio: "Delta Mike 1 2 go ahead.

Carol: "Yeah thanks, is Delta Mike 1 3 available to RV with us on Knowsley Road. Having a few issues with a driver we've stopped for a breath test."

Radio: "Standby. Delta Mike 1 3 from Delta."

Rob, over the radio: "Yeah Delta heard that, I'm making now."

2325hrs.

Rob arrives and speaks to Carol and Zarah.

Rob: "What's the problem?"

Carol: "It's Johnny Bingham in the car, pissed up and high as a kite, refusing to get out and provide."

Rob: "Leave it with me, I'll go in by the passenger door and have a word. If it goes pear shaped he'll be coming out that way."

Rob gets into the passenger side of the vehicle.

Rob: "Listen fella, you need to get out and do what my colleagues are asking you to do."

Johnny: "Listen my mate, I've told those two silly bints out there, nothing is going to happen to me. Even if it gets to court, all the muppets around here worship the ground I walk on, so I'll get let off."

Rob: "Firstly, I'm not your fucking mate and secondly, I don't give a flying fuck who you used to be. Last chance to get out or I'll skull drag you out."

Johnny: "No I won't. Do you not realise who I am?"

Rob reaches over and gets 2 hands underneath Johnny's jaw where there are pressure points and drags him, legs kicking and screaming, out of the passenger side and dumps him on the floor. Carol and Zarah come to assist. Johnny is face down on the floor. Carol and Zarah have managed to get his left arm behind his back. Rob is forcing his right arm behind his back when there is an audible 'crack'. Everybody freezes for a split second and then Johnny starts screaming.

Johnny: "You've broken my fucking arm!"

Rob continues and places the handcuffs on him and they pick him up and place him in one of the Police vehicles.

Rob: "Do you want me to take him as my prisoner now? Just in case I *have* injured him."

Carol: "Do you not mind, Rob?"

Rob: "Nah, par for the course and all that."

Rob: "Delta Mike 1 3 to Delta."

Radio: "Delta Mike 1 3 go ahead."

Rob: "Yeah thanks, will St Helens accept one for a refused breath test please?"

Radio: "Yeah, standby."

2345hrs.

St Helens Custody Suite.

Rob and Johnny are stood in front of the Custody counter.

Rob: "Evening, Sarge. One male arrested for failing to provide a specimen of breath and on suspicion of possession of a controlled drug found in his vehicle after arrest."

74

Rob holds up a small bag of white powder.

Rob: "Circumstances of the arrest are …"

At this stage he is interrupted by Johnny.

Johnny: "This is a fucking joke. I'm a celebrity and this twat has broken my arm. I demand to see a Doctor!"

The Custody Sgt contemplates him for a second and then reaches under the counter and produces a Polaroid photo and shows it to him.

Custody Sgt: "There you go lad, there's a Doctor."

It's a picture of Ken, in a white coat with a stethoscope around his neck giving both thumbs up with a big grin.

Johnny: "You're a fucking tit as well."

Custody Sgt: "Take him straight down to the cells officer, we'll get his details when he calms down."

Rob grabs Johnny by the scruff of the neck and guides him away from the counter.

0045hrs.

In the Doctor's Room in the Custody Suite.

Dr Patel is sat behind the desk as Rob and Johnny enter the room.

Johnny: "For fuck's sake, have you not got any English doctors instead of one who got his qualification in Timbuktu?"

Dr Patel: "And what seems to be the problem?"

Johnny: "I'll tell you what's the problem, if you can understand English properly. This bastard has broken my arm." .

Johnny's right arm does appear to be slightly swollen compared to his left.

Dr Patel: "I understand English perfectly well. Let me examine you."

He comes from behind the desk and takes hold of Johnny's arm and begins to shake it vigorously. Johnny cries out in pain.

Dr Patel: "Nothing at all wrong with this man Officer, you can take him back to the cells."

Rob: "Roger that Doc. Thank you."

Rob puts Johnny in an armlock on his left arm and marches him down to a cell and shoves him in.

Johnny turns around.

Johnny: "Listen mate, this isn't going to get in the papers is it?"

Rob: "Why would they be interested, Johnny? You're not a celebrity anymore, you're just a washed up bag head trying to live off past glories to blag your next fix."

Rob shuts the cell door and Johnny sits down on the bench looking forlorn, feeling sorry for himself.

He whispers, with a sob: "I *am* a celebrity."

0100hrs.

Neil and Chris are on patrol.

Radio: "Patrol to make please, 120 New Edge Street, Sutton. Report of a male threatening to kill his parents.

Neil: "Delta Mike 2 1 making the last."

Chris: "Sounds like an interesting one."

Neil: "They always are on that estate mate. We call it Little Beirut."

0105hrs.

Neil and Chris have arrived on the estate which is poorly built 80's council houses. The gardens are all overgrown and filled with rubbish, the streets themselves are full of broken glass, abandoned settees and mattresses and old cars in various states of decay.

Chris: "I see what you mean mate, never been on this estate before. It's like a scene from Escape from New York."

Strangely, No 120 stands out as it looks like the one well looked after house on the estate; a freshly painted fence, mown lawn and flower borders. It's like a little oasis in a landscape of desolation. In the driveway is an old Ford Cortina that looks like it could be an entrant in a classic car show.

Neil and Chris enter the house and are invited into the living room by an elderly male and female.

Neil: "Hi, I understand that you've been having some trouble with your son?"

Elderly male: "That's right Officer. He's upstairs barricaded in his bedroom because we told him that you were coming."

Neil: "What's been going on?"

Elderly male: "He came out of the Army a few weeks ago after a few years in. We don't know what went on when he was in but he's come home a different lad. Always drinking and then threatening us. For the last 2 nights we've had to sleep down here with the settee against the door so he can't get at us."

Neil: "What's he been threatening to do?"

Elderly male: "He keeps coming in with one of his knives and saying that he'll stab us in our sleep. To be honest, the way he's changed, I really believe that he will if he gets a chance."

Just then Sgt Brodie arrives at scene and Neil fills him in with the information so far.

Sgt Brodie calls the radio room and instructs the rest of the section to attend the scene. He also sends Neil and Chris back to the station to collect everyone's Public Order Equipment.

0130hrs.

All of the section are at scene, apart from Dan who is still stuck on the Front Desk.

Sgt Brodie: "Right folks, the situation is that the lad barricaded upstairs is ex-army but he's come back to civvy life with some issues. He's been threatening to kill his parents during the night and he is believed to have knives in his room."

Ken: "Fucking hell, Sarge. Do you think we should be asking for the ARVs?"

Sgt Brodie: "I'm about to do that Ken but I wanted us ready to deal, just in case we get fobbed off. You know what with us being out in the sticks and the forgotten area of Merseyside."

He then speaks into his radio.

Sgt Brodie: "Delta Sierra 1 2."

Radio: "Delta Sierra 1 2 go ahead."

Sgt Brodie: "Yeah, thanks, can you ask for Armed Response to be deployed to this job in New Edge Street please? Parents are saying that the male has got a knife."

Radio: "Roger, Standby."

A couple of minutes later.

Radio: "Delta Sierra 1 2."

Sgt Brodie: "Delta Sierra 1 2 go ahead."

Radio: "Sorry about this, Sarge. I've spoken to the Force Incident Manager and she is saying that since there has not been a confirmed sighting of a knife by a Police Officer, she will not be deploying ARVs and she is keeping them in the City just in case."

Sgt Brodie: "Roger."

Sgt Brodie turns to the rest of the section raising his arms and shrugging his shoulders.

Ken: "For fucks sake, poor relations again. God forbid they deploy the crayon eaters to a job out here."

Ted, sarcastically: "What do you expect, there's no opportunities to get on the front page of The Echo, guns out and number one rock hard faces on display."

Sgt Brodie: "Come on, to be fair to those I know in the ARVs, if they were aware they'd probably make. But, as per usual we'll have to sort it ourselves."

The section starts to put on their Public Order Equipment - overalls, Nato helmet, body armour, forearm, thigh and shin guards and protective gauntlets.

Ken: "Gotta admit it's sometimes nice to get dressed up as a Stormtrooper though."

Sgt Brodie: "Right, when we get in there, we'll have to force the door and it'll be the Violent Person Tactic from Public Order Training that we'll be using. Ken, Ted and Rob you're the first 3 Officer Team. Neil, Zarah and Carol get yourselves set up as the backup team."

A few minutes later they are all crowded onto the upstairs landing of the house. Ken and Ted have a long clear shield each that they have interlocked and Rob is directly behind them with his arms around their waists, rugby scrum style. They have placed the shields directly against the closed bedroom door. Neil, Zarah and Carol have set themselves up in a similar fashion and are standing near another bedroom door. Sgt Brodie is stood a little farther back.

By this stage even Inspector Bradley has shown up and put his body armour on, although it looks a little ridiculous as it only extends a little below his chest leaving a large expanse of his shirt and belly visible. He is stood by Sgt Brodie but engaged in telling Neil, Zarah and Carol that he used to be a Public Order Instructor.

Sgt Brodie: "Okay Rob, give him a warning."

Rob shouts: "You in the room, this is the Police. Come to the door and bring nothing with you."

There is complete silence.

Sgt Brodie: "Again."

Rob: "You in the room, this is the Police. Come to the door and bring nothing with you."

Again there is silence.

Sgt Brodie: "Okay Rob, try and force the door open."

Rob steps back a little and places his foot against the shields and pushes. The door shatters and splits in half lengthways with one part falling into the room. Rob immediately takes up his previous position.

Now that they can see into the room, they can see there is a small table directly in front of them, a single bed behind that, which looks to have been deliberately moved to the centre of the room. Crouched down behind the bed is a male dressed in combat clothing with his face painted in camouflage colours. He has an air rifle pointed at the shields.

Rob: "Put the weapon down and come to the centre of the room."

The male doesn't respond but fires the air rifle at the shields. Ted, positioned on the right hand shield, takes this opportunity to slide his hand around the shield and flips the table out of the way.

However, at this point, the male vaults the bed with a Samurai sword in his hands and strikes towards the shields. The weapon slides down the edge of Ted's shield and he narrowly manages to pull his hand back just in time.

Ted shouts: "Fucking hell, he's got a sword!"

The male starts to strike at the shields and the sound of the impacts is interspaced with Rob repeatedly shouting: "Put the sword down!"

Then, out of nowhere, Inspector Bradley rushes forward balling: "Right lads, get him."

He barrels into the backs of Rob, Ken and Ted. Not expecting it, they fly forwards into the room and collide with the male. Luckily, he lands on his back on the bed with Ken on top of him. Ken starts to punch him, screaming: "Drop it!" The male lets go of the sword and between them they get him handcuffed.

Ken jumps up to his feet and squares up to Inspector Bradley. "You fucking prick! What the hell do you think you're playing at?"

Sgt Brodie gets in between them: "Back away Ken, now isn't the time."

Inspector Bradley is looking a bit sheepish, realising that he could have caused his staff to be seriously injured.

Inspector Bradley: "Erm, we'll, erm, have a full debrief later."

At this he turns tail and gets out of the house as quickly as he can.

Ken: "Fucking hell, Sarge. We need to start making moves to get rid of that prick. That's 2 fuck ups in 2 nights. If he stays for too much longer I'm gonna swing for him."

Sgt Brodie: "That won't end well, Ken, you know that. I'll start discreetly feeding stuff back to someone higher up that I know we all trust."

Ted and Rob have by now picked up the male, escorted him downstairs and put him in the cage in the back of the carrier.

The section all gather outside.

Ted: "I don't mind telling you when that door opened and I saw a gun, my arse was twitching like a rabbit's nose."

Rob: "Not the only one mate, it was convincing at first glance."

Carol: "What was the boss playing at as well. Apart from how he looked. Did you see that under his body armour? It was like the white band of shame."

Ted: "Yep, he definitely irons his shirts over a wok."

0200hrs.

Ken has popped into the Front Office to see Dan.

Ken: "Alright, cocker, I was expecting a message from you to pick up some scoff."

Dan: "Nah mate, got some butties. You and the Sarge were right, I need to shift a bit. Plus, I'm going away in a few months."

Ken: "Where you off to?"

Dan: "Miami, America."

Ken: "Stuff that, mate. I'd rather drink a pint of crushed glass."

Dan: "What do you mean? It looks dead glamorous."

Ken: "Only the touristy bits, mate. Wander off them and it's a shithole. You'll end up mugged or dead."

Dan: "Behave! Land of the free and home of the brave and all that."

Ken: "I call it the richest third world country on the planet; biggest gap between the rich and poor anywhere. My Mam and Dad went a few years ago. They'd been out for a meal and were leaving the restaurant to walk back to the hotel and the waitress came running out after them saying, 'Don't go that way the bad guys will get you'."

Dan: "Bloody hell."

Ken: "Plus, most of them are as thick as 2 short planks."

Dan: "How so?"

Ken: "Well, a few years ago we used to do our Officer Safety in a local barracks and I was talking to one to the staff there. They'd had some artillery instructors over from America, bit of an exchange thing to see how each other taught things. So the Yank asks him what the process is and the Brit produces a manual and tells him that they have to read this back to front and then sit an exam on it. The Yank has a flick through the book and says it wouldn't work for them."

Dan: "Why not?"

Ken: "He says there's no pictures and 80 percent of their Army can't read. No wonder they can't win a war without us and no wonder there's so many friendly fire incidents."

0300hrs.

Ted and Ken are on patrol.

Ted: "You got me the other night mate with those torches. I'll have to find a better place for forty winks next time."

Ken: "Sorry mate, couldn't resist it."

Ted: "I was speaking to Neil earlier. How do you fancy getting Chris with the old corpse trick later at the mortuary?"

Ken: "What, the old jump out from under the blanket? Brilliant he'll shit himself, I'm in."

0400hrs.

Ted and Ken are in the mortuary and Ken is stripping down to his underpants.

Ken: "When are they due to turn up, this'll be brilliant."

Ted: "About 5 minutes, mate. Jump up onto the slab."

Ken jumps onto one of the metal slabs and Ted diligently ties a label around his big toe.

Ken: "What's the story?"

Ted: "Neil has told him that there was some discrepancy with the paperwork from a job last night so he'll have to check the body over for any injuries."

Ken: "Brilliant."

Ken lies down and Ted covers him with a white sheet, pushes the slab in and closes the door on the refrigerator.

0420hrs.

Ken is lying on the slab shivering. He's coming to realise that he's been had off.

Ken: "Alright Ted, you've got me, open up and let me out."

There is complete silence from outside.

Ken: "Come on, open up. I must've been in here 20 minutes."

Again there is silence from outside.

Ken is really starting to panic now, thinking he's been completely abandoned,. "Come on, it's not funny anymore, it's fucking freezing in here!"

Initially there is complete silence and then - a voice next to Ken.

Voice: "You're cold? I've been here a week."

Ken starts to scream.

After a little while, the door opens and he's pulled out to see all of the Section stood in the Mortuary, wetting themselves laughing.

Ted opens the door next to him and pulls out that slab and it's Rob, all bundled up in cold weather gear.

Ted: "Told you, you'd get your comeuppance."

Ken, starting to calm down: "Yeah alright, alright, you got me there."

0445hrs.

Ted and Ken are still in the Mortuary and are having a brew with the

Mortuary Assistant who the Section affectionately calls Chainsaw.

Chainsaw has one of the bodies rolled out of the fridge at table height.

He is sat behind it with his packed lunch laid out on the sheet.

Chainsaw: "Got a weird one due any second now."

Ken: "What's that, Chainsaw?"

Chainsaw: "Old chap, been dead for a while but locked in the house

with his dog."

Ted: "What's weird about that?"

Chainsaw: "Well it seems the pooch wasn't happy about not being fed.

It's took all the flesh off one of his arms."

Just then the doors to the Mortuary open and the 2 Undertakers come

in wheeling a trolley with a body bag on it.

Undertaker 1: "Anyone want to buy a dog, lovely thing, just don't have

a nap in front of it."

Undertaker 2: "Yep, it's deffo a dog that likes it's Pal."

0450hrs.

Having left the mortuary, Neil and Chris are on patrol. Chris's phone receives a text, which he reads.

Neil: "Who's texting you at this hour?"

Chris: "Remember the girls from last night? I swapped numbers with one of them and she's just sent saying that the there's a party back at the house."

Neil: "There's hope for you yet, lad. Tell them we'll be there in 10."

0500hrs.

Neil and Chris pull up outside the lapdancer's house, get out of the car and knock on the door. The door opens and they go in to what is obviously a party in full swing.

0645hrs.

Neil is asleep in bed with one of the girls and he slowly starts to wake up then glances at his watch. It makes him sit bolt upright in bed.

Neil: "Shit! Chris! Where are you? It's nearly time to go off duty."

Chris starts to curse from another room then bursts into the bedroom.

Chris: "I fell asleep and I can only find my pants."

Neil: "You're having a laugh. I can only find my shirt. We'll just have to go."

Chris and Neil run out of the house to the Police car. Chris has his uniform trousers on and his body armour over his bare upper body. Neil is wearing his shirt and body armour but no pants. They jump into the car and screech off.

Neil: "At the nick mate, we'll have to box clever. If I give you my shirt, leg it upstairs and book off, throw your civvies on and get back to the car with the uniform and I'll go up then."

Chris: "What should I tell the Sarge?"

Neil: "Just tell him I'm looking for a parking space and I'll be up in a bit."

0650hrs.

At the station car park, Chris goes in to the Sgt's office whilst Neil hunkers down low behind the steering wheel in just his underpants and body armour.

Sgt Brodie: "Where's Neil?"

Chris: "Just looking for a parking space, Sarge. He'll be up in a bit."

Sgt Brodie signs Chris's book: "Off you go lad, see you tonight."

Chris nonchalantly saunters out of the Sgt's Office and, as soon as he's out of earshot, he legs it to the locker room and puts on a tracksuit as

91

quickly as he can. He then runs outside and throws the uniform in to Neil, who begins scrambling to put it on.

Neil: "Nice one, Chris. Leave it with me, I'll see you tonight."

Fourth Nightshift.

Sunday

2130hrs.

It's a lovely clear night and the full moon is really bright in the sky. There's no scientific reason for this but every cop knows that a full moon means only one thing for the upcoming shift - absolute fucking bedlam.

Ken has just parked up his private vehicle behind the Police Station and is walking into the rear yard.

He looks up and stares in anger at the moon. He shakes his head and mutters to himself: "Fuck's sake."

2145hrs.

Ken and Dan are in the locker room.

They have found Chris's locker so they proceed to pull it out, turn it upside down and push it back into its original place. They then exit the locker room giggling.

A few minutes later, Chris enters and approaches his locker. He gets his keys out and starts to put them towards the left hand side where the lock would normally be.

He stops, puzzled because there is no lock there and mutters to himself, "I must be knackered."

He then puts the key in on the other side and opens the door. All his equipment falls out at his feet and all around him.

Chris: "Fucking Ken and Dan."

2205hrs.

Ken is in the toilets having a dump.

As he's sitting there, he hears the door open and, after a few seconds, a hand appears under the door holding a CS Canister which is sprayed into the cubicle. He can hear the footsteps of whoever has done it running out of the toilets and the door slamming shut.

Coughing, spluttering and dry retching from the burning sensation in his nose and throat, his eyes burning, Ken musters a scream.

2220hrs.

Ken and Dan are back together as, after the excitement of the last few nights, Ted has volunteered for the Front Office.

Ken is driving and Dan is sat in the back with a prisoner wanted on a Liverpool City Magistrates warrant. They are transporting into Liverpool.

Prisoner: "Which Bizzie Station you taking me to Boss?"

Ken: "We've been told to take you to the Main Bridewell, lad."

Prisoner: "Don't take me there, Boss, fucking awful there."

Ken: "Sorry matey, that's what we've been told."

Dan: "What's the issue with the Main?"

Ken: "It's horrible mate, like a Victorian dungeon. Don't know where they find the bobbies who work there but they're all about 6ft 6in and built like brick shithouses. I feel intimidated just walking in there and I'm on the same side"

Prisoner: "He's not joking Boss. Last time I was in there they chained me to a wall all night."

Ken: "You know the score now lad, keep your mouth shut and do as you're told and you'll be alright."

2235hrs.

They arrive at the Main Bridewell and are buzzed in. As they are walking along the corridor they are greeted by the sight of an enormous Police Officer coming the other way. He's almost a caricature with muscles on top of his muscles. In his hands he is carrying 2 prisoners. He has them handcuffed behind their backs and he has tucked their feet behind the handcuffs. He is carrying them like they are a couple of bags of shopping.

95

Jailor, nodding to Dan: "Offs." Then to Ken.

Jailor: "Ken, good to see you, come down and say hello properly when you've lodged that one. We're just at the end of the corridor."

Ken: "Will do mate, nice to see you too."

The jailor heads off down the corridor, the 2 prisoners looking at Ken and Dan with pleading eyes.

Ken and Dan's prisoner, quietly: "Fucking hell, Boss. I'm shitting myself."

2245hrs.

Ken and Dan have lodged the prisoner and head down to where they've been directed. As they get to the end of the corridor they are greeted by the sight of the Jailor they saw earlier and 3 more equally as big Officers. It's like stumbling across a troop of silverback gorillas.

The floor looks to be highly polished and the Jailors are playing Curling - using the prisoners.

It seems that the object of the game is to slide a prisoner across the floor, getting them as close to the wall as possible.

Ken and Dan watch as one of the Jailors bowls a whimpering prisoner towards the wall. As he slows down, another Jailor walks in front with a brush trying to get as much distance as possible. The prisoner comes to a stop with his head about an inch from the wall.

Whimpering prisoner: "Nice one, Boss"

The Jailor looks up. "Ken, good to see you. Still in semi-retirement out in St Helens."

Ken: "Now don't be like that, you know the score."

Jailor: "Only joking mate, different type of policing out there."

Another Jailor: "Hey, I hear that Bradley has gone out there ?"

Ken: "Our new Boss mate."

Jailor: "Bad luck that. He used to be on my section as a PC. We used to call him FLUB."

Dan: "FLUB?"

Jailor: "Fat Lazy Useless Bastard."

Dan and Ken laugh.

Ken: "You're not wrong there."

Jailor: "Prime example of how brown nosing can move you up the promotion ladder even if you're incompetent."

Another Jailor: "Such is life, turds very often float to the top."

Ken: "Anyway fellas, must dash, St Helens won't be safe without us."

Jailor: "Keep sheriffing out there buddy, always nice to see you."

Ken and Dan walk off.

Dan: "Bloody hell, mate. I've never seen anything like that. How come the prisoners don't complain?"

Ken: "Easy that Dan. They might end up here again."

They head out to the car to go back to civilisation.

2300hrs.

Chris has been put out on foot patrol for a few hours in the Town Centre area. Sgt Brodie is of the opinion that foot patrol is an essential part of learning to be a cop.

Chris is walking along Birchley Street behind the Town Hall and he sees a car coming the other way with only one headlight working.

He decides to stop it so he turns his torch on, directs it to the oncoming car and raises his other hand in the stop sign.

The car, however, speeds up and mounts the kerb heading directly at Chris. He manages to dive out of the way, landing in some bushes.

Chris into his Radio: "83777 scramble, Birchley Street. Just attempted to stop a car and it's tried to run me down and made off towards Standish Street." He passes over the registration number.

Over the radio: "Delta Mike 1 1 making", Delta Mike 2 1 making"

Radio: "83777."

Chris: "83777 go ahead."

Radio: "Yeah, thanks Chris, that vehicle comes back as a green Vauxhall Corsa with no current keeper."

Ken and Dan screech to a halt next to Chris.

Dan, out of the window: "Jump in Chris, we'll have a look around for it."

Chris gets into the back of the car.

Ken: "You okay mate?"

Chris: "Bit shaken."

Ken: "Let's see if we can find the bastard."

They drive around the area for a bit then hear: "Delta Mike 2 1."

Radio: "Delta Mike 2 1 go ahead."

Rob's voice: "Thanks, we've found the vehicle abandoned behind the St John's Ambulance Centre off Standish Street."

They head to the location and find Rob and Carol with the car.

Everyone gets out and look around the vehicle. The bonnet is still warm and the driver's door has been left open. There is also a large bag of Chinese takeaway on the front passenger seat and a strong smell of alcohol in the car.

Dan: "Whoever it was is obviously plastered."

Ken: "Thing is with no current keeper, they just have to lie low and report it stolen in the morning. We'll never prove they were driving then."

Chris: "Bastard tried to take me out."

Rob looks over at Ken: "Some summary justice in order?"

Ken: "Bastards got to pay somehow."

Rob goes into the car and pops the bonnet and then proceeds to empty all the takeaway food over the front and back seats.

Ken lifts the bonnet, gets a multi-tool out of his pocket and proceeds to cut every wire, pipe and cable that he can find in the engine bay. He then closes the bonnet.

Ken: "Fucker won't be using that again."

Chris: "Won't they just claim on insurance?"

Ken: "If they haven't registered it, I doubt they've got insurance. That'll all come out of their pocket if they even come back for it."

Dan: "Come on Chris, we'll drop you back off at the Nick and you can sort yourself out a brew to calm down a bit and change your underwear."

2320hrs.

Ken and Dan have dropped Chris off at the Police Station and are now having a quick drive through the Town Centre.

They pull up outside The Bank Public House. On the door is Jimmy, a former heavyweight professional boxer who had the dubious distinction of having never won a bout.

Ken: "Now then Jimmy, how's things?"

Jimmy comes over to the car, he's had that many punches to the face that he looks like he fell out of the ugly tree and hit every branch on the way down.

Jimmy: "Alright Ken, just about to turf everyone out."

Ken: "No bother tonight then?"

Jimmy: "Never any bother when I'm on the door."

He then does a bit of shadow boxing, throwing out a couple of jabs.

Ken: "Behave Jimmy, you're the only professional boxer I know who used to have sponsorship on the soles of his boots."

Jimmy laughs. "You're a knobhead, Ken."

Ken: "Always good to see you getting some work Jimmy, you're one of the good ones. We'll see you later."

At this they drive off slowly, continue around the corner and park up at the corner of Church Street and Bridge Street.

Ken: "Someone got me before."

Dan: "How do you mean?"

Ken: "I was in the bogs dropping the kids off at the pool and someone sprayed me with CS from under the door."

Dan, laughing: "Easy target that mate, everyone knows you go for a dump straight after parade."

Ken: "Got to mate, never shit in your own time."

Dan: "How do you mean?"

Ken: "I have a crap at least twice a shift and it adds up mate. By the end of the year, the job has paid me a few days just for having a shit. Over the course of 30 years, it's about 8 months pay."

Dan: "Haha, brilliant mate. I'll keep that in mind."

Ken: "There's times when I've been on parade and I've been touching cloth."

Dan: "Eh?"

Ken: "The turtles been that curious, it's popped its head in and out a couple of times."

Dan laughs.

Ken: "Mind you I used to work with a bloke who used to average about 5 craps a shift. By the time he finishes, they'll have paid him about 3 years wages just for sitting on the bog."

Dan: "Can't believe that before with Chris."

Ken: "I know. Think we went for the best option though. Even if the bastard is traced tomorrow it probably wouldn't get to the charging stage."

Dan: "Yeah, the Justice system is a joke."

Ken: "Tell me about it. I always say our job is to get them locked up and gather as much evidence as we can. After that, it's job done and out of our hands."

Dan: "How do you mean?"

Ken: "Well, the first hurdle is the Crown Prosecution Service. They'll have a look at it and weigh it up to see what they think their chances of winning at court are. If it's a low percentage in their view, they'll bin it off. Not interested in Justice, just their win figures."

Dan: "I know what you mean there. I've had a few good jobs knocked back."

Ken: "Then it gets to court and at that point it's all a game between prosecution and defence solicitors and barristers. You see them furtively meeting in corners or rooms on the court landing making deals."

Dan: "How so?"

Ken: "I was in court the other week with a bang on Grievous Bodily Harm. It met all the criteria for it, textbook example, and if the witness and me would have been allowed to give evidence I'm 100% certain he would have been convicted. But, oh no, the barristers met up and did a deal. If the offender pleaded guilty to a lesser Actual Bodily Harm, the CPS would accept it. A win for both barristers; CPS get a conviction, Defence get a lesser sentence for their client so both of them look good."

Dan: "I never realised that went on."

Ken is on a roll now.

Ken: "And then it's pot luck with which Judge you get. Some are pro-police, some are pro-defence, and some are totally removed from reality and think only of themselves."

Dan: "Go on." He loves hearing Ken giving his opinions.

Ken: "Another job I had at Crown Court. First day of the trial, everyone is there, three bobbies, the victim, six prosecution witnesses plus all the ones for the defence and the jury too. The Judge comes in, sits down and as soon as the case is announced he stops the proceedings."

Dan: "What for?"

Ken: "I kid you not these were his exact words – 'I see the trial is listed for 5 days. I'm afraid I'm playing golf on Friday so we'll have to adjourn'. True as I'm sitting here!"

Dan: "You're joking."

Ken: "I wish I was."

They both sit there for a little while contemplating the losing battle they are fighting day to day.

A group of girls walk past the Police car obviously the worse for drink. One of them stands directly in front of the car, pulls her top down and shakes an enormous pair of breasts at them.

Ken and Dan are wide eyed.

Dan: "Bloody hell, they're like a dead heat in a Zeppelin race."

Ken: "Never mind that, look at the fucking size of her nipples. They're like monkey's thumbs."

She then turns her back to them, lifts up her skirt and bends over. She isn't wearing any underwear and she spreads her cheeks at Ken and Dan while all the other girls cheer. They then all walk off laughing.

Ken: "Don't see that very often."

Dan: "She didn't bother trimming the back did she?"

Ken: "Telling me, looked like a goat's eye winking at us."

Dan: "Everything looks better trimmed."

Ken: "Including your own, Dan?"

Dan: "Yep, everything shaved."

Ken, laughing: "Fucking hell, I bet it looks like the last chicken on the shelf at the supermarket."

Dan: "Knobhead."

Soon, across the road from them they see a male staggering along. He stops, looks down at the floor and starts kicking at a loose piece of block paving.

Ken: "What's this fucking idiot up to?"

Dan, looks at the controls in the Police car: "Don't think we're in stealth mode mate."

By this time, the male has managed the pry out a block and stands looking at the window of a nearby shop.

Ken: "Don't you fucking do it, don't you fucking dare."

The male then throws the block at the window, which smashes, and then throws his arms up and runs around in circles as though he's just scored a goal.

Ken: "Fuck's Sake."

Ken and Dan jump out of the Police car and run across the road and grab the male, who starts to struggle violently with them.

They manage to get him down on the floor. He's face down, Ken has his knee on his shoulder and his right arm straight up in the air in the Ground Pin position. Dan starts to do the same with his left arm so that they can get him under control and handcuff him.

Dan has just settled his knee down and got the male's arm near enough vertical when he starts to wriggle about. Dan falls backwards and the male's false arm comes completely off in Dan's hands. He lands on his back and then sits up still holding the arm, looking at in disbelief for a few seconds, genuinely thinking that he's pulled off a real arm.

Ken: "Stop dicking about and help me."

Ken by this stage has managed to get a handcuff onto his real arm. Dan jumps up and goes to help.

The male is still moving about, trying to break free.

Dan: "How the fuck do we cuff him?"

Ken, puffing and panting: "Get the other cuff through his belt."

They manage to get his arm into the small of his back and fix the other cuff to his belt and then sit him up.

Ken, into his radio: "Delta Mike 1 1 to Delta."

Radio: "Delta Mike 1 1, go ahead."

Ken: "Thanks, can you see if St Helens will accept one adult male for Criminal Damage please?"

Radio: "Yeah, will do."

0030hrs.

Neil and Zarah are together in Delta Mike 2 1 and

parked up in Exchange Street opposite The Lincoln Square Public House which is emptying out.

Zarah: "Are we just parked up here so you can have a blimp at all the women?"

Neil: "Don't be daft Zarah. There's usually trouble outside here at kicking out time."

Zarah: "Seems quite low key at the minute."

Neil: "Not for long, the old spider senses are tingling. It's going to go off like a bottle of pop in a minute."

They watch for a little while and then, sure enough, two males start fighting with each other. Neil and Zarah jump out of the car and run across the road shouting, "Police! Stop fighting!"

The males, however, continue to trade punches. Neil rugby tackles one to the floor, landing on top of him.

Zarah approaches the other male and he takes a swing at her with his right fist. She blocks it then grips his wrist with her left hand, steps in and throws him over her shoulder in a spectacular throw. She then holds him down in a wrist lock.

However, by this time, they are surrounded by approximately 20 males, screaming at them to let the 2 prisoners go.

They both draw their CS canisters, holding their positions and shouting, "Get Back or I'll spray!"

Neil, into his radio: "Delta Mike 2 1. Con Requires Assistance, Lincoln Square, Bridge Street."

The radio repeats this while Neil and Zarah keep the baying crowd back, shouting at them and threatening them with being sprayed.

Within a minute they can hear sirens and then Rob and Carol coming speeding around the corner; the crowd starburst and scatter. Rob and Carol get out and assist them with the prisoners.

Neil: "Thank God you were close by. For a minute then I really thought we were going to get a good kicking."

Zarah: "Yeah, always a relief to hear the sirens getting closer."

Rob: "Yeah, I always say the sirens can have 1 of 3 effects as they get closer when there's a fight. One, they all stop fighting and run away. Two, they all stop fighting and all want to tell you at the same time why they *were* fighting. Or three, they stop fighting with each other and want to fight with you. Lucky it was the first tonight."

Neil: "What was that you did to him though, Zarah? It was like watching an action movie."

Zarah: "Did you not know? I'm a black belt in Judo, done it for years."

Neil: "Bloody hell I wouldn't want to mess with you."

They pick the prisoners up and place them in the two separate cars.

0100hrs.

Ken and Dan are back out on patrol after lodging their prisoner.

Radio: "Any patrol to make to Haresfinch Road please, report of a male walking down the road naked and masturbating furiously."

Ken: "Delta Mike 1 1 making."

Dan: "How the fuck do you masturbate furiously?"

Ken laughs: "Dunno mate, maybe you shout at passers-by as your pulling one off."

0105hrs.

They arrive at scene at the same time as Rob and Carol in Delta Mike 2 1.

Sure enough there is a naked male walking down the road, masturbating vigorously.

They all get out and as they are approaching him Ken says: "Thought you'd show up Carol, comparing it to Neil's?"

Carol: "Knobhead."

They get to the male, who stops walking.

Ken: "Alright mate, are you okay?"

The male doesn't respond, just moans, looks them all in the eye and continues masturbating.

Ken: "Have you took something mate?"

He still doesn't respond and continues as he is.

Ken: "Well, for whatever reason it looks like he's having some sort of mental health crisis."

Dan: "How do you know that?"

Ken does a double take. "Fucking hell Dan, it's not exactly normal behaviour is it."

Rob has been busy calling the Control Room for an Ambulance to attend.

The male starts to stare at Carol with laser like focus and quickens the pace that he is masturbating, his hand almost becoming a blur.

Dan: "Bloody hell, he'll pull it off if he's not careful."

Ken: "He likes you Carol, give him a bit of encouragement."

Carol: "Sod off, Ken."

The male suddenly lets out a roar and erupts, ejaculating like Mount Vesuvius. Some of it goes onto Dan's jacket.

Dan leaps back: "Shit, I've got jizz all over me."

The male sinks down and sits on the floor spent and mumbling to himself.

The Ambulance arrives and Ken updates them on what's happened. They approach the male, help him up and he goes with them placidly. As they are putting him in the back of the Ambulance, Dan approaches them.

Dan: "Don't suppose you've got any spare wipes?"

Paramedic: "Why? What's up mate? Did you approach him prematurely?"

Laughing, he hands him some antiseptic wipes.

The other Paramedic pops his head out of the Ambulance. "Fucking hell mate, you should see the state of his knob, it's red raw. It looks like a rustic chorizo sausage."

Ken: "I'm not surprised with how tightly he was choking the chicken before."

0145hrs.

Neil and Zarah are on patrol.

Neil: "They don't often put us together, Zarah."

Zarah: "You're right there, don't know why."

Neil sees an opportunity. "So, erm, how's your love life?"

Zarah: "You don't need to be getting any ideas, Neil. I won't be succumbing to your charms."

Neil: "Haha, no worries, always worth a try."

Radio: "Patrols to make 38 Eskbank Avenue, Moss Bank. B and E now. Report from a neighbour that they have seen a male forcing the front door about 20 minutes ago."

Neil:"Delta Mike 1 2 making."

Zarah: "Twenty minutes ago? Why didn't they phone then?"

Neil: "Some people just don't want to get involved, probably left it for a bit and then their conscience got the better of them."

0150hrs.

Neil and Zarah arrive at the scene. It's an affluent looking area and the house is a large 1930's detached. Sure enough, the door is open with signs that it's been forced.

They both draw their batons and enter.

Zarah: "Police! Is anybody there?"

Someone's trying to shout, it's high pitched but garbled and seems to be coming from a room in the downstairs section.

Neil and Zarah follow the sound and, in a back lounge, find an elderly lady. She's been tied to a chair and gagged. She also has severe facial injuries, her nose is bloodied and her face swollen on one side. Zarah looks down at her hands and can also see that several fingers appear to be bent back and broken.

Neil: "Look after her, I'll search the rest of the house."

Zarah starts to console her and untie her.

Neil comes back. "All clear."

Zarah: "Can you tell us what has happened?"

The elderly lady tells them that she was asleep on the settee when a male burst in, tied her up and forced her to reveal where her jewellery was.

Neil listens and then: "Delta Mike 1 2."

Radio: "Delta Mike 1 2, go ahead."

Neil: "Can confirm that there has been an Aggravated Burglary. Offender described as a white male, early 20's, St Helens accent, wearing a dark tracksuit with a distinctive white stripe down the legs and believed to have stolen a quantity of jewellery including several gold chains and a sapphire ring. Can you contact the Night Detective and circulate to patrols please?"

Radio: "Roger, will do."

Neil: "Further to the last, call the Ambo as well, the elderly female occupant has been beaten, severe facial injuries and broken fingers."

0155hrs.

Rob and Carol have been listening as this comes out over the air.

Rob: "Sounds like he's tortured her, the bastard. If I get my hands on him we'll see how tough he is, an old woman like that."

Carol: "I won't be stopping you, I'll be joining in."

115

They have started making to the area and are driving along Carr Mill Road.

Rob suddenly shouts, "Stop the car! I think I saw someone."

Carol slams on and Rob jumps out. He rushes down a dirt path leading towards Carr Mill Dam, a local waterway.

Carol parks the car up and follows the general direction that he went.

Rob has caught up with the male on a bridge over the water. He matches the description including the joggers with a white stripe down the sides.

Rob: "Stand still and show me your hands."

Male: "Alright, Boss. Okay, I've not done nothing."

Rob: "You match the description of a male responsible for a burglary nearby so I'm going to search you. Have you got anything in your pockets that could harm me or you?

Male: "Nothing on me, Boss."

Rob conducts a thorough search of the male and finds a ring with a large sapphire stone.

Rob: "You thieving bastard, You're under arrest on suspicion of burglary."

Male: "Should have made sure the old bag couldn't talk."

Rob loses it and grabs hold of the suspect.

Carol has just now caught up and is coming onto the bridge. She is greeted by the sight of Rob dangling the male over the side, holding him by his ankles.

Rob, shouting: "Where's the rest of it, you robbing bastard!"

Male: "Fuck off pig."

Rob: "You fucking tortured that old woman, now tell me where you've hidden the rest of the jewellery or I'll drop you."

Male: "You wouldn't fucking dare."

As Carol gets next to him, Rob let's go of the male's ankles and he falls screaming into the water.

Rob and Carol look over the side and they can see that the male has narrowly missed one of the concrete stanchions and is now treading water.

Just then, there is a cough from their left. They look over and can see a fisherman sat on the bank, calmly looking up at them. He nods solemnly at them and says: "Officers."

Rob and Carol rush down to the bank and direct the male to swim over to them, which he does as it looks like he's had enough now. Rob pulls him out and handcuffs him behind his back.

Rob turns to the fisherman: "Everything okay, sir."

The fisherman is very well spoken, "Everything is fine, Officer. I wasn't having much luck tonight but I see you caught a big one."

Burglar: "Did you see that mate? If I make a complaint, will you be a witness?"

Fisherman: "Hm, I saw and heard everything so it's probably best that I demonstrate rather than speak at this point."

At that he suddenly lunges forwards and kicks the burglar hard between the legs. "Thieving bastard!"

The burglar doubles over screaming in pain.

Fisherman: "Right, Officers, I'll pack up and be on my way. I was never here and good luck finding the rest of the old lady's things."

He wanders over to his equipment and starts to pack up.

Rob: "Delta Mike 1 2."

Radio: "Go ahead Delta Mike 1 2."

Rob, "Thanks, one male detained on suspicion of Burglary, he tried to escape by jumping into the Dam but we've got him. One item of property recovered but could do with a dog patrol to maybe have a search of the area."

Radio: "Roger."

Over the radio: "Delta Whisky 5 4, I heard that, I'm on my way."

Ten minutes later, PC Gary Marsden arrives with Police Dog Barney.

Rob updates him on the route he took and they then head back to the Police car whist the Dog Patrol searches the area.

When they are travelling to St Helens Police Station they hear over the Radio.

"Delta Whiskey 5 4."

"Delta Whiskey 5 4 go ahead."

"Yeah, thanks, we've located a small black bag containing a quantity of jewellery."

0200hrs.

Ken has decided to set up Inspector Bradley to prove to what he's really like. The whole section and the radio room are in on it.

Dressed in all dark clothing and a balaclava, he's sitting in the patrol car with Dan.

Ken: "Right mate, drop me off and then make yourself scarce. Come and pick me up when it's all clear."

At this, he gets out of the car in a country lane and goes behind a hedge.

0205hrs.

Radio: "Delta Sierra 1 1."

Inspector Bradley: "Go ahead."

Radio: "Yeah thanks, sorry about this Boss but can you make a job for us please?"

Inspector Bradley: "Is no-one else available?"

Radio: "Sorry, Boss, everyone else is tied up on jobs or with prisoners."

Inspector Bradley: "I suppose so, what's the job?"

Radio: "Thank you, it's a report of an intruder dressed in all dark clothing at Lane Ends Farm in Clockface."

Inspector Bradley: "Yeah, will Do."

0210hrs.

Inspector Bradley arrives at scene with blue lights and sirens on, a tactic often deployed by the work shy to make sure the offenders can hear them coming and escape so that they don't have to deal with them.

Inspector Bradley gets out of the car and starts walking along the country lane, shining his torch about.

As he gets close to him, Ken pops up from behind the hedge. Inspector Bradley looks directly at the figure in the balaclava and promptly turns around, gets back in his car and drives away.

Inspector Bradley: "Delta Sierra 1 1."

Radio: "Delta Sierra 1 1, go ahead."

Inspector Bradley: "Yeah, thanks, I've had a look around and it's area searched no trace."

Ken, meanwhile, is on his phone to another operator.

Ken: "He's just got in his car and fucked off. Looked straight at me and did nothing, send him back."

Radio: "Delta Sierra 1 1."

Inspector Bradley: "Go ahead."

Radio: "Yeah, thanks, the informant has been back on. Says you must have missed the suspect as he's still there. Can you go back please?"

Inspector Bradley: "Erm, yeah, will do."

Inspector Bradley re-attends and approaches the same bit of hedge and again, Ken pops up."

Inspector Bradley: "Police, stay where you are!"

Ken turns and starts to run across the field and Inspector Bradley starts to give chase. Ken isn't running very fast and soon realises that Inspector Bradley isn't gaining on him.

Inspector Bradley: "Police, stand still!"

Ken slows down to give him a chance to catch up a little but Inspector Bradley doesn't close the gap. He just raises his knees a bit higher in that silly run that people do but don't appear to go any faster.

Ken does this for a little longer and then runs off out of sight.

Inspector Bradley: "Delta Sierra 1 1."

Radio: "Delta Sierra 1 1 go ahead."

Inspector Bradley, over exaggerating his panting: "Yeah, thanks, disturbed the male and gave chase but he's managed to get away from me. I'll have another quick look around to make sure he's gone."

Radio: "Yeah, roger."

Inspector Bradley makes his way to the car and drives around for a bit.

0300hrs.

Ken, Dan, Carol and Rob are in the Refreshments Room at the Police Station.

They've all just opened their packed lunches and have settled back into their seats.

Carol: "No takeaway tonight then Dan."

Dan: "Nah, fancied some butties for a change."

The door opens and Gary Marsden comes in with Barney. Barney is the biggest German Shepherd you'll ever see, huge head, huge paws and the size of a small pony.

Barney plonks himself down in the centre of the room, looking at them all, head on paws and tail wagging. Barney loves St Helens cops, as far as he's concerned they're all his mates and he loves being around them.

Carol: "Thanks for that before, great find."

Gary: "No problem, he's a good un. I've not met you before, you're one of them wobblygobs aren't you?"

Carol: "Wobblygobs?"

Gary: "You know, from Liverpool. There's another name for them, can't think of it at the minute."

Carol: "Scousers."

At this Barney raises his head, ears pricked.

Gary points at Carol: "You hear that Barney, she's a scouser."

Barney jumps to his feet directly in front of Carol barking and snarling aggressively at her.

Gary: "Barney, enough, she's okay, she's one of us."

Barney stops barking, cocks his head to the side looking at Gary. Then looks back at Carol, wags his tail and gives her a boop on the knee with his nose. Then he plonks himself back down.

Ken is laughing his head off. "Brilliant trick you've taught him there, Gary."

Carol: "What is it with you lot about people from Liverpool. It's a great city, not a shithole like around here."

Ken: "You're joking aren't you? Where do you live Carol?"

Carol: "Bootle."

Ken: "How many people from St Helens live on your street?"

Carol: "Eh? None."

Ken: "Well I live in St Helens and there 5 of them from Liverpool live in my street and the bastards won't move back."

Carol: "Piss off Ken, some of the houses I've been in around here."

Ken: "You forget, Carol. I've worked both and, even though scousers look down on us St Helens folk, I've been in far worse houses in Liverpool."

Carol: "Are you being serious or just trying to wind me up?"

Ken: "Straight up, when I worked in Liverpool there some houses there that I used to wipe my feet when I left them, they were that bad."

Carol: "Which is better to work though?"

Ken: "Obviously, I'd say here but they all have their own particular difficulties; for example, violence. In general, St Helens folk are bigger and don't mind a bit of a scrap but they'll forget about it afterwards or try and shake your hand and apologise. In Liverpool they're generally smaller but nastier, won't think twice about jumping in to gang up on you or stamp and kick you when you're down. I'd say Kirkby is the worst, they've got the size of St Helens people but the nastiness of some scousers."

Carol: "So you're sticking with here then?"

Ken winks at her: "Yep, my purpose now is to try and keep the scousers out of St Helens. But I suppose you go with whatever fits best."

Carol: "Still say I'm proud of my city."

Ken: "You sound like one of them celebrities."

Carol: "How do you mean?"

Ken: "You know, those professional scousers on TV. 'I'm proud of my city'. Oh yeah mate, where do you live then? Erm, Cheshire."

Inspector Bradley enters the room carrying a bag and manages to squeeze himself into one of the seats.

Inspector Bradley: "Busy one out there tonight isn't it."

Ken: "Yeah, Boss. Full moon innit."

Inspector Bradley> "I had to deal with a job myself before."

Ken:"Yeah, heard that one come out, we were stuck in the Custody Suite. What happened?"

Inspector Bradley: "Intruder at Lane Ends Farm. I disturbed him and gave chase but he was a little bit too fast for me."

Ken: "Yeah, some of them are like whippets aren't they?"

Inspector Bradley: "You're telling me, 10 years ago I'd have had him. I used to be a sprinter you know. I could have represented the country but decided to join the Police instead."

Inspector Bradley then gets a foil wrapped oblong parcel out of his bag. It's a 12inch baguette stuffed with meat. He places one end at his mouth and gnaws through it in seconds.

He then struggles to stand to his feet; "Well, no rest for the wicked, got some portfolio stuff to box off."

He leaves the room and they sit there in silence for a bit.

Then, Gary: "Fucking hell. How fast did he devour that nudger?"

Ken: "Took me back to my youth that did, it was like watching Scooby Do devour one of his snacks."

0400hrs.

Ken and Dan are back on patrol.

Dan: "I was reading Force Orders before. They've advertised a secondment in it for 12 months with the United Nations Police. Haven't you done that?"

Ken: "Yes, mate, in 1999. I went to Kosovo for 12 months."

Dan: "Bet you saw some horrible stuff there."

Ken: "It was just picking up the pieces mate. The most traumatising bit was the two day medical in the selection process before I went over."

Dan: "How do you mean?"

Ken: "Well, on day one they have to check your prostate and all that."

Dan: "That's not too bad, good to know all is okay."

Ken: "Well there is that but there I was on the bench, lying on my side with my knees up towards my chest and this doctor comes in. I swear to God he had hands like fucking shovels and fingers like Cumberland sausages. He holds up two of the fuckers and tells me to relax and shoves them up me bum and has a root around. Next day, there were about 15 of us sat around having breakfast and no one was talking. Everyone felt violated."

Dan: "Fucking hell mate."

He thought for a while then said quietly: "I suppose it's worth giving it a miss to avoid that."

Radio: "Patrols, please, to make the Rainford Bypass, report of a fatal RTC."

Ken: "Delta Mike 1 1."

Dan: "Thought you hated Traffic jobs mate?"

Ken: "Ah, pick and choose mate. Show willing on this one. If it's a fatal, Traffic will take over with the paperwork etc, we'll just first aid it then hand over."

Five minutes later they arrive at scene but the Dog Patrol had got there before them.

Ken and Dan block the road with their car and jump out, leaving the blue lights flashing.

As Ken is approaching Gary shouts: "Watch where you're standing Ken, there's brains all over the road."

Ken looks down and can see bits of grey brain matter strewn across the road and he starts to get that 'death' smell in his nostrils.

He can see there is a car parked up a little further along the road and a male sat in it with his head in his hands.

Ken to Gary: "Drink Driver mate?"

Gary: "No mate, poor bugger was just on his way to work and this other poor bugger stepped out in front of him."

Ken: "Bloody hell, not what you'd call a good start to his day."

Gary: "Come and look at the body mate, there's something bugging me about it."

They walk a little further up the road to a grass verge on the left hand side and there is a body lying on the grass.

It's mangled. They can tell it's a male but that's about it. The face has twisted around so it is now positioned where the right ear would be. The front of the skull is open and there is a large hole where the brains have come out. The rest of the body is all twisted at odd angles.

They both look down at it for a minute.

Ken: "You're right mate, something is off."

Gary: "I know, can't register what it is though."

They contemplate the body for a bit longer before it dawns on Ken what is wrong.

Ken: "Fuck me mate, where's his other leg?"

Gary: "Shit, best find it."

They walk further along the grass verge and find the severed leg. Bizarrely, it's standing upright.

Gary: "Is it bad taste to say he almost landed on his feet?"

A few minutes later the first traffic patrol arrives in big estate and an Officer gets out all dressed in motorcycle leathers. He is big and overweight.

Traffic Officer: "Now then Ken, you lazy bastard, what's the score?"

Ken: "Alright, Bill. Why are you in leathers in a car? One of your kinks?"

Bill: "Knobhead. I went out on the bike till midnight and then swapped."

Ken: "Not much of one for the environment are you?"

Bill: "What?"

Ken: "Fuck me mate, they must have killed 4 cows to make your leathers."

Bill: "Dickhead> What's gone on?"

Ken and Gary fill him in on the accident as other traffic patrols arrive.

Bill: "Right, leave it with us."

Ken, Dan and Gary start walking back to their cars.

Dan: "Love to be in traffic, driving around in a fast car all shift."

Ken: "Up to you mate but you'd be constantly looked down on by the rest of us."

Dan: "Why's that?"

Ken: "You know what they say about Traffic."

Dan: "What?"

Ken: "If you don't want to fight wear a white hat."

0420hrs.

Neil and Zarah are driving along Prescot Road and they pass a male walking along sipping from a beer bottle.

As they pass, he launches the bottle at the Police car shouting: "Fucking pigs." The bottle hits the rear light cluster on their vehicle, causing it to smash.

Neil slams on the brakes and they both jump out. The male turns around and starts to run, hotly pursued by Neil and Zarah. He is really fast and rapidly starts to open up a gap.

If you've ever had to run wearing body armour and an equipment belt you'll know that it's like carrying an extra stone to a stone and a half of weight. If you don't catch them in the first 60 metres you probably never will, unless you are ultra-fit.

131

The male, because he's so far ahead, stops running, turns and takes up a wide stance. He then proceeds to give them the 2 fingered salute with both hands, laughing.

He waits until they are about 20 metres away and then suddenly turns and sprints away, head down but promptly runs head first into a lamp post knocking himself unconscious.

Neil and Zarah catch up and, giggling, put him in handcuffs and into the recovery position.

0530hrs.

Ken and Dan are on patrol.

Radio: "Delta Mike 1 1."

Ken: "Delta Mike 1 1 go ahead."

Radio: "Can you make to Blackbrook Post Office please? Report of a burglary."

Ken: "Will do."

0535hrs.

Ken and Dan arrive at scene and are let into the post office by the Post Master.

He leads them through the shop and into the back and they can see that the safe is wide open and empty.

Post Master: "Second time in 5 years this is. They've bypassed the alarm and took about five grand."

Ken: "Did you hear anything?"

Post Master: "Not a bloody thing, just had a funny feeling and came down to check the office. I'll tell you what though, I don't think it's a coincidence that we were done 5 years ago and the bastard that did it got out last week."

Dan: "Who was that then?"

Post Master: "Jed Smith. Last time, the Police searched his house and found all the money hidden in the washing machine."

Ken can't resist. "In the washing machine? What was he doing? Laundering it?"

The Post Master looks at Ken for a few seconds and then bursts out laughing.

Post Master: "It's a good job I've got a sense of humour mate. Quick that was."

Dan and Ken take the report of Burglary and organise for the Night Detective and Scenes of Crime to be informed.

They then get back in the car and head off.

Ken: "Hopefully that's the last job of the night."

Dan: "Yeah, looking forward to a couple of days off before late shifts."

Ken: "Fucking hate working afternoons. All we deal with after 5pm is feral kids running riot."

Dan: "Fucking horrible little rugrats that hate us."

Ken: "You know why they hate us don't you mate?"

Dan: "Go on."

Ken: "It's cos we're the first people who pull them up and say, you can't do that! Their parents have never bothered, as far as they're concerned the little cherubs can do no wrong."

Dan: "I get you. Bit of parental responsibility would go a long way."

Ken: "Bloody hell Dan, you almost sounded educated there for a second, but yeah, whenever we take them home the parents are usually stoned."

0650hrs.

In the Sgt's Office. Sgt Brodie, who has had to cover Custody all night, is sat at the desk with enough tumbler glasses for the section. As they enter, he opens his desk drawer and brings out a bottle of Whisky.

Sgt Brodie: "The Inspector went off at half 3 because he's got a round of golf with the Chief Super later today."

Ken: "Alright for some eh, hell of an early dart he's given himself."

Sgt Brodie: "Yeah, apparently he's his mentor. If anyone spots them on the golf course, later, all you'll see are his golf shoes coming from the Chief Super's arse cos he'll be brown nosing that much."

Ken: "I take it you've made up your mind on the new boss then Sarge?"

Sgt Brodie: "Yep, just try to keep yourselves out of the shit for a few months. He'll be off on some project by then to get evidence for promotion. He wasn't happy when he went off though."

Ken: "How come?"

Sgt Brodie: "He came back down to his office after scoff to find someone had left a great big turd in his hat."

Ken: "Brings a whole new meaning to the phrase shit for brains."

Sgt Brodie: "It's not funny, Ken. He was steaming."

Ken, laughing: "Steaming, good one Sarge."

Sgt Brodie: "Was it you?"

Ken: "Can't blame this one on me Sarge. I was there when he was having scoff."

Sgt Brodie: "I don't think he'll let this one lie. We've not heard the last of it. He was buzzing before he found it though, reckons he's come up with a brilliant idea that'll put him on the map."

Rob: "What's that then?"

Sgt Brodie: "He was talking about that job last night where we all had to get kitted up and how long it took to get riot shields to the scene. He reckons with just leg pads and shorter shields, carried in the boot of the car, there's enough protection for almost anything."

Rob: "That's fucking stupid."

Sgt Brodie: "He doesn't think so. He spent the beginning of the shift sawing down 2 shields to make them fit."

Rob: "Does he not know that it'll make them weaker and they'll shatter with one hit?"

Sgt Brodie: "Nope, apparently not. They're in the back of the Inspectors' car and he's left a report on the Chief Inspector's desk."

Rob: "Well at least it's an original idea, not the usual re-inventing the wheel that bosses usually come up with."

Ken: "That should speed up getting him moved then, she's not one to suffer fools gladly."

Sgt Brodie: "You should know Ken, you dated her for a while."

Ken: "Spot on Sarge, voice of experience here."

Sgt Brodie pours the Whiskys and hands them out: "Another successful set of nights, no one injured and all going home safe. Cheers everyone."

They all raise a glass.

The End (maybe).

About the Author

Dave Leigh served 30 years in Merseyside Police - 15 years on the frontline and then 15 years in a training role where he ended his career as the Lead Officer for Safety Training.

Since retiring he has become a Director of No Duff UK, www.no-duff.com, a not for profit Community Interest Company which provides help and support for serving and former members of Armed Forces, Emergency Services, NHS, Prison Service and Animal Welfare Staff who are suffering from Mental Health issues due to their service.

He was the Police Advisor for the BBC Drama 'The Responder' and lives with his wife and son in the Northwest of England.

Printed in Great Britain
by Amazon

21520210R00088